Find out how the adventure continues!

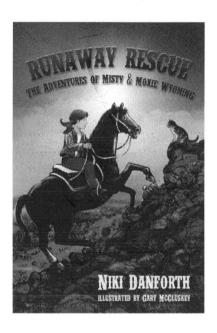

Avaliable on Amazon

Color the adventure as you read!
Both Available on Amazon

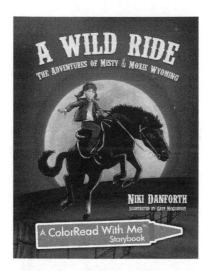

A ColorRead With Me™ Storybook of *A Wild Ride*

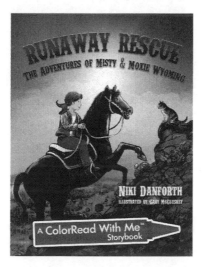

A ColorRead With Me™ Storybook of *Runaway Rescue*

A Wild Ride

The Adventures of
Misty & Moxie Wyoming

By

Niki Danforth

Illustrated by

Gary McCluskey

Publisher: Pancora Press, New Jersey

Book Design: Donnie Light eBook76.com

Cover art: Gary McCluskey
http://garymccluskey.carbonmade.com/

Cover Design: KT Design, LLC ktdesignllc.com

Enjoyment Level: 7-12 years old, but content appropriate for children as young as 5 years old

Dedicated to

Misty of the Darwin Ranch

and

Moxie Wyoming Sigel
who loved and cared for
Misty during her final years

In Memory of
Brad Hendricks
1941-2014

When it was time for the real Misty to retire from the Darwin Ranch, Brad, the inspiration for the character of Grandpops in the novel, came up with the brilliant idea that this feisty little horse should move to his daughter and son-in-law's ranch in southeastern Wyoming. That is where a rich friendship developed between Brad's beloved granddaughter, Moxie Wyoming Sigel, and Misty, Queen of the Darwin Herd.

Horse Talk

(in order of appearance)

Mare: an adult female horse or pony, at least four years old

Corral: a pen or enclosure for animals, such as horses and cows

Blacksmith: a person who trims a horse's hooves, and also makes, fits, and attaches horseshoes to the hooves

Cutting horse: a saddle horse trained to separate a selected cow from a herd and prevent it from returning to the herd

Roundup: circling around animals to gather them together

Snowies, or *Snowy Mountain Range:* a mountain range in southeastern Wyoming

Palomino: a horse or pony with a golden coat and white mane and tail

Paddock: a fenced area near a barn where animals wander safely

Foal: a baby horse or pony less than a year old

Trot: move at a quick, steady pace

Lope: faster than a trot and slower than a gallop

Gallop: the fastest speed a horse can go

Colt: a young male horse or pony, less than four years old

Filly: a young female horse or pony, less than four years old

Gros Ventre Mountains: (pronounced "Grow Vaunt") part of the Central Rocky Mountains in western Wyoming

Chapter One

"It's my birthday!"

Moxie Wyoming Woodson popped up in bed, her brown hair sticking out every which way.

"And I hope, I hope, I hope that Mom and Dad will give me my very own horse."

Moxie blinked at the early morning light streaming through the window. It landed on her favorite poster of a wild Mustang herd galloping through a canyon.

She listened to the rooster crowing, rubbed her eyes, and jumped out of bed. Today was also the start of summer vacation, and she didn't want to miss a second of it.

In a flash, Moxie brushed her teeth, used her fingers to comb her shoulder-length hair into loose pigtails, and threw on some jeans and a tee-shirt. She heard a barking noise and rushed downstairs.

"There you are, Bunkie-Bunkie!"

Moxie plopped down at the bottom of the staircase and nuzzled the family dog, a lovable golden retriever mix from the local pound.

"Oh, my Bunker!" He licked her nose, and Moxie giggled. "Are you wishing me happy birthday?" She scratched behind his ears and hugged him. "You are *sooooo* cute!"

1

She looked up at a large painting hanging in the front hall. It was a portrait of her great-grandmother from long, long ago, dressed head to toe in pink cowgirl clothes, sitting on a beautiful black horse.

"I wonder if I'll ever grow up to be a champion like you, Granny Rose." Moxie sighed. "Then I could be extra-special, too, like you." She hopped up and hurried into the kitchen with Bunker.

Moxie added milk to a bowl of cereal her mother had set on the table, and gulped it down. She rehearsed a short speech for her father, reciting it to Bunker. The dog tilted his head while she practiced, as if he were listening, but she knew he was really more interested in what she was eating. Placing the bowl on the floor for Bunker to lick, Moxie dashed out the door.

She saw her dad by the barn loading gear into the bed of his truck. She tiptoed over and noticed how his shaggy dark hair stuck out every which way. She loved that he looked like her when she got up in the morning, but he got to look that way all day long. *I guess it's 'cause he's a grown-up,* she thought, *and he doesn't have a mom making him comb his hair.*

He was also wearing his favorite faded denim shirt and tan work pants, held up by wide red suspenders that Moxie had given him for Christmas. She quietly reached up from behind and playfully snapped the suspenders, surprising him. "Daddy, what's up?"

"Hey, Moxie Wyoming! Happy birthday!" Laughing, Mike Woodson swooped up his daughter for a good morning hug and kissed her on the cheek. His unshaven face tickled her.

"Daaad-dy!" She wiggled loose. "Where are you going?"

"I just got a call from Officer Clem Brown over at the highway patrol," he said. "He thinks wild horses may have broken through some of our fencing near the road to town." Her dad checked the hitch connecting the back of the truck to a trailer. "I'm worried our own horses will get loose, so I want to get over there and repair the fence."

"Me, too," Moxie said, looking hopeful. "You can help me saddle up, and I can ride with you."

"Now, darlin', I don't have the right horse for you...at the moment," he said, glancing at the trailer.

"But, Daddy, that's just what I want to talk to you about. Even though we're not celebrating my birthday until tonight, I'm already ten *this morning*..." Moxie tilted her head down and launched into her speech. "And if I had my very own horse—which I hope I will *sooooon*—I could ride with you and help with your chores. Like fixin' the fence."

Her father walked to the back of the four-horse trailer. "Moxie Wyoming, we'll just have to see—"

"We'd have more daddy-daughter time," she interrupted, and beamed her widest smile at him. Chuckling, he closed the doors of the trailer.

"Hold it, Daddy. Where's your horse?" Moxie asked. "Aren't you riding over to fix the fence?"

"Like I said, kiddo, the broken fence is close to the road, so I don't need a horse to get there." Her father climbed into the truck and started the engine. "Anyway, when I'm finished with the fence, I'm driving on to Laramie."

"But what's in Laramie? And why do you need the trailer?" Even as Moxie asked, it dawned on her that he'd only take the trailer if he needed to pick up a horse, maybe a *birthday* horse? "Daddy—"

"Later, squirt." Waving to her, he put his foot on the gas and the truck rolled down the road.

Moxie climbed aboard one of the ranch's all-terrain vehicles and propped her dusty, brown cowboy boots on the handlebars. If her father was picking up a horse for her, wouldn't he take her along, especially on her birthday?

"I guess it's not happening..." She rubbed the small scar on her elbow. "I'll probably be an old lady before I get a horse. And that will look just weird."

~~~~~

Later that afternoon, Moxie sat on the step by the kitchen door next to a purring gray barn cat as her father pulled up. Her chores were done. She had also gathered eggs in the chicken coop, eaten lunch, and been waiting for what seemed like forever. Now he was back. Finally.

"Hey, Dad, what's in the trailer?" Moxie called out. She grinned, hopeful again. "My birthday present?"

"How'd you know, kiddo?" Mike Woodson smiled at his daughter as he climbed out of the truck.

"Sure, Dad. Right." She figured he was kidding.

He unlatched the back door of the horse trailer and stepped into the dark. Moxie could hear her dad moving around inside, speaking quietly to someone. With growing excitement, she walked over, carrying the cat in her arms.

"Come on, girl," he urged gently, as he came out. "Come see your new home."

Expecting to see a fine-looking young horse stride down the trailer's ramp, Moxie stopped in her tracks and dropped the cat when she finally got a look. This could *not* be her birthday present. It had to be a terrible mistake.

Chapter Two

Moxie watched her father lead off the trailer what she thought was the saddest excuse for a horse ever. The animal's black coat was so gray-flecked, that he—or was it a she?—looked more gray than black, making it look old. But the horse's most noticeable feature was the steepest swayback Moxie had ever seen. It swooped down and made the animal's belly hang as low as low could be.

"What's up with that horse, Dad? You could skateboard down one side and up the other," she sputtered.

"Moxie Wyoming, you cool it," he said and smiled. "This little mare is yours!" The barn cat meowed and ran off. *That cat feels the way I do,* Moxie thought.

"Daddy, is this a joke?" She took in his expression which said *no.* "Can I even ride this horse?"

"Yes, you can," he answered.

"Aren't there any others in Laramie? This one looks really old and kind of ugly—"

"Hold it there, young lady. She can't ride fast anymore, but she'll get you where you want to go around the ranch." He gave his daughter a stern look. "I did go to Laramie to pick her up, but Misty—that's her name, by the way—is from much further away, all the way across the state. She's retiring from the Darwin Ranch near Jackson."

"But Dad—"

7

"Now, listen, Moxie. Misty's a legend at that ranch and a real favorite of the Darwin guests," he continued. "Even though she's more than thirty years old, she's been queen of the herd out there forever."

Moxie's face drooped in disappointment. "Why'd she—"

"Every morning at the Darwin, the wrangler rounds up the horses for the guests. And Moxie, Misty was *always* out front, leading the herd back to the corral at a full gallop."

He scratched Misty's neck. "And even though the guests didn't ride her much anymore, she was still the boss of the Darwin corral."

"So why'd she have to come here?" Moxie pushed out her bottom lip.

"Your grandfather's a good friend of the owner of the Darwin, and they decided it was time for Misty to retire."

Her dad must have noticed her quivering lip, and he said in a gentle voice, "Grandpops and the owner thought our ranch would be a nice place for her to live out her golden years."

"But I can't ride her in the barrel races at the rodeo like Pickle's cousin." Moxie sniffled. "Or Granny Rose."

"That's true. Misty is pretty much retired," he said. "Hey, birthday girl, stop your whining. One day you'll have a horse for barrel racing. In the meantime, Grandpops and I thought you'd be the perfect candidate to take care of this little mare."

Moxie didn't feel convinced, and sniffled again.

Her dad pushed his hat back from his forehead. "Now, Moxie, everybody knows how you love animals. Every time I turn around, you've brought home some injured critter or abandoned little one you find around the place. I should call you Doctor Moxie, the way you like to take care of animals."

He nodded toward the gray cat as it darted past them into the barn. "Why, there goes Pie. You took him in during that snowstorm last winter. Remember?"

He offered Misty's lead rope to his daughter. "Come on, squirt. Don't you want to meet her?"

Moxie noticed that the old horse looked bored and sleepy, as if she didn't want to be there, either.

Moxie shuffled over, frowning and kicking up dust with her cowboy boots. Reluctantly taking the lead rope, she stood sighing heavily before her dad as he made the introductions. She did happen to notice Misty's one white sock on her left hind leg.

Her dad noticed the leg, too. "Looks like Misty's lost her shoe on that hoof. We'll have to get the blacksmith over to take care of that."

"Yeah, whatever," Moxie said, glancing at the horse's face. She was surprised to see Misty's brown eyes wide open and looking straight at her.

Then Moxie watched something peculiar. While the horse's left eye stayed open, her right eye closed and then snapped open again.

Is she winking at me? Moxie wondered and looked at her dad. But he was busy examining Misty's hoof that was missing a shoe.

Moxie looked back and the little horse did the winking-thing *again* and smiled at her, showing all her teeth. *This is definitely weird,* Moxie thought.

~~~~~

That night, Moxie huddled under her blanket in bed. She watched her long, lean mother cross the room in a few graceful strides to turn off the lamp. Moxie could hardly wait for the growth spurt that would put her on the road to her mom's almost six-foot height.

"That was a delicious cake you made for my birthday. Thanks, Mom." Moxie reached up to play with the thick strawberry-blond braid that hung down over her mother's left shoulder. "But please make sure Bunker stays away from my cake, 'cause chocolate will make him sick..."

Jane Woodson tucked the light cotton blanket around her daughter. "Now, Moxie Wyoming, I know this birthday didn't work out quite the way you'd hoped," she said. "But give it time. You'll feel better about things in a few days. You'll see." She kissed Moxie on the forehead and left the room.

Moxie pulled an envelope out from under her pillow. She flicked on a flashlight and reread the letter from her grandfather.

Dear Moxie Wyoming,

She may not be much to look at, and I'd have to admit she's even kind of homely. But I promise you that Misty is one special mare. You can't even begin to imagine how this old girl will change your life, even though she's a senior citizen, like me. Just give her a chance and let her into your heart.

Your dad and I figured you were the perfect gal to look after her because you love helping animals. Why, I remember when Bunker arrived at your house, scared to death. And now look at him. What is it you like to call Bunker? A regular love bug? And it's all because of how you took care of him.

By the way, Misty's going to need you as a friend, 'cause I'm sure she'll miss her buddies at the Darwin Ranch. There's Bandit, Misty's son...he looks just like her but light brown, and he's kind of taking over now that his mom isn't around anymore to lead the herd. There's huge Hector, Misty's protector. There's the spoiled peanut butter-colored pony named Heber...

Moxie Wyoming drifted off to sleep, thinking about all the different horses at the Darwin Ranch. In her dream, she did not see Misty, who would have probably slowed her down and gotten in the way. Instead, Moxie sat on top of a beautiful, frisky, golden-colored horse with a white mane and tail, proudly leading the herd across a meadow.

Chapter Three

Moxie Wyoming loved going to the rodeo in Laramie with Pickle Turner. The two had been like brother and sister since first grade, when Pickle's father, Willie, came to work for Moxie's dad at the family's Moose Creek Ranch.

Their first meeting had been memorable. Moxie had filled a glass jar with crickets, hoping to surprise the skinny kid with wild, curly, blond hair. Pickle thought Moxie just wanted him to look at the bugs, but Moxie surprised him by dumping them all over his head.

Instead of yelling the way most kids would, Pickle had jumped up, laughing that the crickets tickled. Moxie couldn't believe Pickle's reaction. To top things off, Pickle had bravely picked up some of the insects and thrown them back into Moxie's hair. That sealed the deal, and they became best friends forever.

Now, Moxie sat in the rodeo bleachers with Pickle and his mom, Carol Turner, cheering on Pickle's older cousin, Sue. They watched Sue Turner race her horse around barrels set up in a clover-leaf pattern. Sue rode a special cutting horse that she had trained to separate cows from a herd of cattle.

More than calf roping, team roping, or bull riding, this rodeo event, barrel racing, was Moxie's favorite. She could imagine herself chasing around those barrels in record time, winning first prize just the way her Granny Rose had done so long ago.

If I just had the right horse, instead of that old Misty, she thought, *I could practice to be a real champion.* She squeezed her eyes shut. *Maybe my wish will come true.*

The cheering of the crowd turned her attention back to the rodeo as Sue Turner finished her ride in record time. Moxie Wyoming jumped to her feet. "You know what? I've been wishing on my lucky star, my horseshoe, and my rabbit's foot for a great horse. I'm going to practice riding around barrels every day. And before you know it, I'll ride in the rodeo and be a champ just like Sue."

"You're not old enough, Moxie. You have to be a teenager," Pickle piped up.

Moxie gave him a stare that would stop a grizzly in its tracks. But Pickle got that look from Moxie at least five times a day, so he was used to it.

Mrs. Turner squeezed Moxie's shoulders. "I believe you've just turned ten—"

"My dad says that's double-digits," Moxie interrupted. "So I guess I'm almost a teenager!"

"Slow down there, pardner!" Mrs. Turner said. "You and Pickle— please don't be in such a hurry to grow up."

Why do people keep telling me that? Moxie Wyoming smiled just the same.

~~~~~

After the rodeo, the kids wandered among the different pens and corrals comparing the horses and bulls. They looked through one fence to admire an enormous black bull with deep, dark eyes.

"Don't stare at him, Pickle," Moxie giggled. "He'll give you the stink eye and put a hex on you."

Pickle quickly looked away. "Okay..."

"Hey, Clem Brown!" a voice called out from a nearby pen. "Why aren't you on duty, drivin' 'round in your fancy new highway patrol cruiser?"

Moxie looked up in time to see a man in a highway patrol uniform shaking hands with two cowboys. *So that's Officer Clem Brown,* she thought, the one who'd called her dad and told him about their broken fence. She nudged Pickle.

"How are you Jenkins boys doing?" The officer smiled at the two cowboys and then spoke quietly. "Hey, what's been happening since that roundup went bad near Rock Springs last month?" Both cowboys looked surprised and uneasy.

The highway trooper went on. "Jeb, I heard you were almost arrested by some sheriff's deputies over that way." Moxie and Pickle's eyes grew big as they listened in.

"Whew! That was a close call," the cowboy in the dusty-brown hat said, looking around to make sure no one overheard. Uncomfortably shifting his eyes away from the uniformed officer, Jeb mumbled, "But hey, big buddy—"

"Don't look so worried, guys," Officer Brown interrupted in a low voice. "I just had a talk with your friend over there, Tony Olsen. He told me we could, uh, *help* each other if you're planning more...well..." The highway patrolman also looked around, but he seemed to be searching for the right words.

Pulling on Pickle, Moxie ducked down, although they could still see the three men through the fence. The trooper went on. "I might be interested in, you know, lending a hand, if you get something going."

Jeb and the other cowboy studied the lawman for a long moment. "Well, well, you do surprise me, Officer," Jeb said in a quiet voice. "So, you know Tony Olsen?" He paused a moment. "We just might be gettin' ready for a new roundup, this time in the Snowies."

Moxie Wyoming jabbed her friend hard in the ribs, and Pickle almost yelped. Moxie quickly put her finger to her lips, showing Pickle he had to stay quiet.

Jeb looked at the cowboy in the charcoal-gray hat next to him, who nodded back. "My brother Frank and I have been thinkin'," he said. "There's one person we haven't found yet—"

"—who could help us," Frank spoke up, but also in a low voice. "If we decide to do a roundup, that is."

Peeking through the fence, Moxie thought Jeb and Frank Jenkins sort of looked tough. Their hats were pulled low over their faces, that were covered with scruffy whiskers.

"Do you guys have enough help for the roundup?" Officer Brown asked.

Jeb laughed. "I'm sure there'd be plenty of ranchers 'round here who'd line up to join us, but we ain't there yet."

"Keep this to yourself, Clem," Frank said. "We're buildin' a corral, not far from Centennial. It's secret, okay? Nobody knows about it." His voice got even quieter, but Moxie could certainly still hear. "It's the perfect pickup spot for our buyer. He's payin' big bucks, by the way."

"Hey, I'm over that way all the time," Officer Brown said. "Even though I'm new around here, I know the area you're talking about. How can I help?"

"We'll let you know right before if the roundup happens, 'cause if it does, some trucks will be drivin' to and from the corral," Jeb said. "That way you can be a sort of lookout."

Moxie and Pickle couldn't believe what they were hearing. Anxious, they glanced around carefully, not wanting to be discovered.

"And we'll pay you good money for keepin' the nosy neighbors away," Frank added, covering his mouth with the edge of his hand as he spoke.

"Great," the officer said. "I may be an officer of the law, but these are just a bunch of dumb old horses and I could use the extra cash."

"Remember, don't talk about this with *anyone!*" Frank reminded him.

"We don't want to get arrested for makin' some money." Jeb smiled crookedly. "Just because some people think we're breakin' the law."

"And you definitely want to keep your fancy highway patrol job, so it's better if you don't get caught helpin' us." Frank jokingly fake-slugged the officer's arm. "Get my drift, buddy?"

Wide-eyed over what they had just heard, Moxie and Pickle peeked through the fence right above the back of the black bull. Officer Brown and the two cowboys walked away slapping each other's backs and laughing.

Pickle rubbed his hands over the goose bumps on his arms. "That sounded scary."

"They sure didn't want anybody else to hear them," Moxie said.

"I'm glad they didn't see us." Pickle shuddered. "Are they planning a crime?"

"Yeah, they could be," Moxie said, noticing Pickle's shivers and the bumps on his arms. "You heard what they said about breaking the law and not getting arrested. So whatever they're planning, it must be no good."

"Isn't the officer supposed to be one of the good guys?" Pickle asked.

"My dad told me sometimes even good people can do bad things," Moxie answered.

The two stood up, and Pickle shook his legs out nervously. "They were talking about a roundup. What do you think they want to round up?" he asked.

"And a secret corral," Moxie added. "They said they're building a secret corral near Centennial."

"That's close to *us*..." Pickle's nervous voice cracked.

"I wonder where exactly, and what for?" Moxie looked around. "Maybe for cows or horses?"

"You mean they're going to steal someone's cows and horses?" Pickle asked.

Moxie Wyoming scrunched her face in thought. "Hmmm. Remember, they said other ranchers would probably join their gang. So they wouldn't steal ranch cows and horses."

Then Moxie's eyes lit up. "Hey, maybe we can find out what's going on and why this corral's supposed to be a secret. We can be like cowboy detectives!"

Pickle didn't look very happy about that idea.

Chapter Four

While cleaning Misty's stall the next day, Moxie Wyoming thought a lot about the suspicious conversation she and Pickle had heard the evening before. She tried to figure out how to review the case as if she were a real detective.

First, she needed to go places to investigate and find out exactly what Jeb and Frank Jenkins were planning—was it a crime? She wasn't old enough to drive, so how could she follow them around to see what they were up to? If only she had a better horse...

Moxie paused every now and then to sneak a look at Misty. She tried to keep in mind what Grandpops had written about how special the horse was. Dad had even called her the queen of the herd. But Misty sure didn't look special or act like a queen. Finally, Moxie stopped sweeping and looked directly at the swaybacked horse.

"Just thought you might like to know I had a dream about the ranch where you used to live, Your Majesty." She leaned against the pitchfork she had been using to spread around clean straw. "I was on my very own horse, a pretty palomino. She didn't have any gray hair like you."

Misty looked at her and then shifted her gaze to the pitchfork Moxie was leaning against. The mare snorted, smiled with all her teeth showing, and then flicked her tail. The pitchfork wobbled, bounced up, and tipped over, causing the girl to lose her balance and topple into the straw.

Moxie Wyoming coughed from the dust. "Excuse *me*, Your Highness." Sniffing and embarrassed, she struggled to her feet. "What kind of hocus-pocus was that?" She glanced around the stall, a little bit spooked. Was someone playing a trick on her? Misty now had both eyes closed.

Moxie picked up the pitchfork and stomped out.

A loud snore erupted from the stall, and Moxie stopped. *That poor excuse for a horse is taking a nap,* she thought. *How rude!*

She hurried over to where they kept their equipment and dropped the pitchfork, knocking it into some buckets. She hoped the clanking noise would wake up Misty. It didn't.

Then Moxie heard Pickle calling her. She raced out of the barn, leaving behind the little snoring mare.

~~~~~

"Pickle, hold on tight," Moxie yelled from the all-terrain vehicle as the two of them raced along a dirt road past Pickle's house and toward the highway.

"Slow down, pleeeease!" Pickle shouted back, sitting behind Moxie. "You're driving way too fast! If my dad catches us—"

"Where'd you see them?" Moxie Wyoming slowed the four-wheeler just a little. "Are you sure they were the same two guys?"

"It was definitely those guys from the rodeo, the ones we saw talking to the officer," Pickle insisted. "They were fixing a tire on their truck right near the Deer Crossing turnoff."

Moxie quickly turned the handlebars, steering the machine to the left to avoid a deep hole, and their helmeted heads lightly clunked each other. "Okay, that felt weird..."

"Mox-ie Wy-o-ming!" Pickle yelled. "I don't like the way you drive! My dad said I'm only allowed to go slow—"

"Okay, okay." Moxie slowed down some more. "If we can find those Jenkins guys, maybe we can discover their secret corral."

"But, Moxie, you know we're only allowed to ride on the road between my house and your house. We can't go near the highway. My parents will ground me for sure, and yours will, too, if we drive any further," Pickle shouted. "Anyway, we shouldn't go looking for them, they'll hear us coming."

Moxie ignored her friend and continued driving. Pickle rolled his eyes and gave in. He slumped down on the back, hanging onto Moxie.

As they raced on a dirt road alongside the highway, Moxie tried to spot the truck. She carefully hit the brakes as they neared a side road. The ATV came to a stop, but there was no truck in sight.

"My mom and I were coming home, and this is exactly where I saw them changing the tire." Pickle then pointed to the side road. "I wonder if they drove down the turnoff over there."

"I don't see anything down that road, you know, like dust from a truck," Moxie said. "How much of a head start do you think they got?"

"Don't know, maybe fifteen minutes—"

"Let's go." Moxie Wyoming gunned the engine.

The two friends sped along Deer Crossing, which took them over hills and down hidden gullies. They drove into the foothills below the Snowies and watched for anything suspicious.

As they drove over one more rise and sailed down the other side, Moxie and Pickle spotted a truck parked among the trees on the right. They also saw two cowboys working inside a partially built corral. The ATV cruised to a stop.

From the vehicle, Moxie and Pickle watched Jeb Jenkins use a noisy chainsaw to cut wood. Frank Jenkins pounded wood posts into the ground with a sledgehammer. "Should we try to get closer?" Moxie asked over the noise of the saw.

Just then Jeb spotted them and turned off the saw. "Hey, you two! What are you doin' over there?!" he yelled, putting down the saw to move in their direction. He smiled. "Hey, Frank, check it out."

Startled, Frank whipped around, seeing them, too. He dropped the sledgehammer, hopped the fence, and also started in their direction, grinning. "Do you kids wanna take a better look?"

Moxie shivered; he was creepy.

"GO, GO!" Pickle shouted, pounding Moxie's back.

"Come on. We're just buildin' a corral for our pack horses," Jeb called out.

Moxie just wanted to get out of there fast.

With Pickle hanging onto her like glue, Moxie nervously revved the engine, turned the ATV around, and took off. She glanced back while racing over the hill, terrified but excited that they'd found the secret corral, just like real detectives.

By the time they made it back to Moose Creek Ranch and pulled up to Moxie's barn, the kids had calmed down.

A blacksmith was hunched over with Misty's white-socked leg propped between his knees. He nailed a new horseshoe onto the hoof.

"Whose horse is that?" Pickle asked. "She looks kinda broken down."

"It's a long story." Moxie sighed.

"Hey, is she staring at us?"

But Misty looked at Moxie, not Pickle, and when only the girl looked back at her, the little horse winked.

Did Misty just wink at me again, like the other day? I'm sure that was a wink! Moxie winked back this time.

"What's wrong with your eye?" Pickle asked.

"It's just an itch."

Misty gave Moxie another secret wink, this time adding a circle-*swoosh* with her tail.

Chapter Five

A big, wet tongue slurped Moxie Wyoming's cheek as she lay sprawled on the rear seat of her dad's pick-up truck. Her eyes popped open, and she found herself staring straight into Bunker's face. He gave her another slurp, this time on her nose.

"Enough, Bunker." Moxie took the back of her hand and wiped her face. "I wish Daddy would hurry up in the feed store. I'm hungry, and it's lunchtime."

She heard the sound of footsteps nearby. Before she could sit up to greet her father, the footsteps stopped, and the back of the vehicle next to her dad's clunked open.

"Everybody's talking about those M-M-Mustangs over in the Snowies," a teenager's voice said with a nervous little stutter. Moxie perked up at the mention of wild horses, since Mustangs were her very favorite.

"I know. Stan was just telling me about it inside the feed store," a man with a gravelly voice answered. Moxie very slowly raised her head to peek through the window. She saw two people loading supplies into the truck parked alongside her dad's.

"Well, they're too c-c-close to our place." The teen sneezed, and then added, "I'd like to get rid of them all."

Moxie Wyoming, shocked by what she'd just heard, tried to get a better look. The older girl's black hair was in a ponytail, and her dark, reddish-brown cowboy hat cast a shadow over her face.

"There may be a way." The man slammed the truck's tailgate shut.

A way to do what? Moxie worried. *Get rid of the Mustangs? Who was this guy, anyway? Was he the teenager's boss, or maybe her father?*

She noticed the cowgirl didn't stand very straight as she stared at the ground. Moxie's mom was always pulling back her shoulders, telling her that good posture showed the world she felt good about herself.

The two got in their truck and backed out of the parking space. As they drove off, Moxie read the words *Curly T Cattle Ranch, Centennial Valley, Wyoming* on the side of the vehicle.

Bunker barked happily as Moxie's father and a young store clerk carried out several bags of horse feed. Before Moxie could hop out to help, her dad said, "Sit tight, kiddo. We've got it." He and the clerk loaded the bags into the truck bed. "Thanks for your help, Ben."

"No problem, Mr. Woodson. See you around." The teenager went back into the feed store.

"Okay. What'll it be? Burgers or a B-L-T for lunch?" her dad asked, as they drove off.

"A burger, please," she said. "I'm starving!"

~~~~~

After lunch, Moxie Wyoming strolled out to the corral to water Misty. She saw her father and a bow-legged, mustached cowboy fixing a hinge on the corral gate. The cowboy was Willie Turner, Pickle's father. The two men were absorbed in their work and didn't notice Moxie near the barn.

"...there's been talk about a wild Mustang herd running loose in the Snowies," Willie said.

"Yeah, Stan Sheffer mentioned it when I was at his feed store earlier," Moxie's dad answered, as he and Willie lifted the gate back onto its hinge. "How big of a herd?"

"You know Matt Larson at the Moore Ranch?" Willie asked. Moxie's father nodded, and the ranch hand continued, "Well, when he was passing through a few days ago, Matt thought he saw about fifteen to twenty Mustangs led by a palomino-colored stallion."

Moxie Wyoming held her breath. *Fifteen to twenty Mustangs! I wish one of those was here instead of that old Misty in the barn.*

"I wonder if they were the same Mustangs that ran through one of our fields and damaged our fence," Moxie's dad said. "Anyway, what do you think will happen to them? You know how a lot of ranchers feel about wild horses."

"Yeah." Willie swung the gate back and forth to check the new hinge. "Some of those guys would like to see the Mustangs just disappear, if you know what I mean."

Disappear? Disappear why? Moxie Wyoming's eyes grew huge. *And where to?* She rushed into the barn and dashed to a window to look out at the Snowies. She tried to imagine the herd of wild Mustangs running through the canyons of the mountain range.

Her gaze settled on Misty, who stood peacefully in the paddock. The mare's eyes were closed, and Moxie heard a snore. "Hello. It's the middle of the day, and you're asleep! I don't believe it," Moxie harrumphed.

Misty's brown eyes opened wide and she stared straight at the girl, then let out a huge snort. Moxie jumped as if she'd been caught sneaking a cookie, and laughed nervously, kind of embarrassed. She looked over at a plastic container filled with horse snacks, then back at Misty. "You like treats?"

Misty's eyes flashed, and she pounded her right hoof twice.

"Okay, okay..." Moxie Wyoming gawked at the little horse. "I get it, I think." She grabbed a handful of nuggets from the container and walked into the paddock toward Misty. "Is that pounding with your hoof some kind of trick signal or something?" The horse's eyes were closed, and she was perfectly still. *Asleep again,* Moxie thought. *Come on!*

"Wake up, Misty." Moxie carefully held out several of the treats in her palm. "I've got something for you!"

Misty opened her eyes. She looked at the nuggets, then at the brown-haired girl who was holding them, and carefully took them with her lips.

"Oooh, that tickles," Moxie giggled, giving Misty more.

As Misty crunched on the goodies, Moxie stroked her neck. "Uh, maybe you're not so ugly, you know, the way I thought when you first got here," she said in a grumpy voice. Then Misty sneezed, spraying Moxie. "Eeeew!" the girl screeched, but she laughed, staring at the little horse. "You are kinda funny-looking in a cute-weird way."

As Moxie Wyoming walked back to the barn, Misty fell in behind her, interested in more of those tasty treats.

~~~~~

"Pickle, how's your new puppy?" It was late afternoon, and Moxie closed the fridge. She poured cold lemonade from a pitcher into two glasses.

"You mean Flopsy?"

"What kind of a name is that for a puppy?" Moxie asked. "That sounds like the name of a rabbit."

"Well, she's the same color as my rabbit, so who cares? She likes her name, and so do I." Pickle beamed. "I'm so glad you rescued her from the grocery store."

"Yeah, well she looked so sad and lost and hungry in that parking lot all by herself." Moxie put the pitcher back in the fridge. "I tried to find the mama, but I didn't see one. And Mom said I had to find a home for her because we already have enough animals around here."

"I've wanted a dog forever, and Flopsy's perfect. Thank you for giving her to me."

Moxie took a drink of her lemonade. "Hey, I wasn't being a snoop, but I listened to your dad tell my dad that a herd of wild Mustangs is running around the Snowies."

Pickle nodded. "I know. I heard him tell my mom about them last night." The boy reached into an old-fashioned cowboy-shaped jar for some fresh-baked chocolate chip cookies. "Mmmm. These smell good! How many do you want?"

"Two, please." Moxie grabbed the glasses of lemonade. "Follow me."

"Where we going?" Pickle piled five fat cookies onto a paper towel.

"To look at pictures of Mustangs." Moxie's voice drifted down the hallway, and Pickle hurried out of the kitchen after her.

They entered her parents' office, and Moxie carefully placed the lemonade on a table in the middle of the room. "Did you know that some people out there can't stand Mustangs?" she said. "I heard these two people saying awful things about them today. Boy, how can anybody hate horses?"

"I don't know," Pickle said. "They'd have to be pretty mean."

While Moxie looked through a bookcase in the office, Pickle gazed at the walls filled with photographs of Moxie's parents during their competitive riding days. Many blue ribbons and belt-buckle-awards from competitions surrounded the pictures.

"These buckles are so cool!" Pickle stood transfixed in front of one extra-gigantic silver buckle. "Your dad won this?"

"Yeah, at the rodeo in Jackson," Moxie said. "That's also where he met my mom one summer when she was on vacation from Connecticut...and then they got married...and then they bought this ranch...and then they started raising cutting horses."

"Cool," Pickle said, still staring at the belt buckle.

"Here, I found it." Moxie brought a large book over to the table.

The friends sat quietly munching cookies and looking at the book together.

"It says here, *There were two-million wild horses in North America by 1900.* Wow, I never knew that. That's a lot of horse poop." Moxie Wyoming guffawed at her own joke.

Pickle rolled his eyes and continued reading out loud. "*There are a lot fewer wild horses today, maybe even less than 50,000.* Okay, that's really, really sad."

"Look at this picture of this brown horse," Moxie said. "It says here she's a 'lead mare.' See, it also says, *A band, or family, of Mustangs needs an older lead mare to take the horses away from danger. She's the* one the others in the herd trust to lead them to safety. The stallion brings up the rear, protecting the Mustangs from danger."

"They're kind of like a people-family with a mom and a dad," Pickle said.

The kids studied the photographs closely. "They sure are nice-looking," Pickle said. "Too bad your new horse doesn't look like one of these."

"Well, that's just 'cause she's not so young anymore," Moxie said in a matter-of-fact tone. "I'm sure Misty used to be nice-looking, too. Maybe she needs some makeup or something..."

"That's goofy," Pickle said. "A horse with makeup..."

Spinning in the desk chair, Moxie Wyoming leaned back and closed her eyes. "Boy, I sure wish I could see those Mustangs up in the Snowies!"

Chapter Six

"Misty, did you see that little guy dive under the ground over there?" Moxie Wyoming giggled. "Those critters are so cute! And funny!"

Since her birthday, Moxie and Misty had been spending more and more time together. At the moment, the two walked inside a fenced-in pasture as tiny ground squirrels called chislers poked their heads up from burrows in the dirt and then darted back underground.

"There goes another one! Misty, look, that chisler's huuuge!" Like all the others, this big one dove into a burrow beneath the ground.

Misty put her face close to one of the holes, and Moxie kneeled down to watch. The horse tapped the ground lightly with her right hoof and then snorted softly into the hole.

Soon a small furry head peeked out, looking at Misty. The little chisler reached up, rubbed noses with the mare, then caught sight of Moxie and dove back into the hole.

Moxie stared at her horse. "Misty, I don't know what kind of magic you have, but that was amazing!"

"Moxie Wyoming!" her dad's voice called. He came around the side of the barn.

"How are you and your little mare doing on this fine day?" he asked. "Are you trying to see how close you can get to a chisler? I used to do that all the time when I was a kid."

"Misty and I got close to that last one." Moxie guided her horse toward her father. "Daddy, I have a question."

"Sure, kiddo," he answered. "Shoot."

"I heard you talking to Mr. Turner about some wild Mustangs in the Snowies."

"Yep, that's true."

"And you thought maybe they were the same wild horses that broke our fence," Moxie said. "Does that mean you don't like Mustangs?"

"Not at all," he said. "And we're really not sure how the fence got broken. Why do you ask?"

"Mr. Turner said some of the ranchers want those Mustangs to just disappear. What did he mean? Disappear how?"

Her father didn't answer right away. Moxie's brow furrowed with worry. "Why can't the Mustangs stay in the Snowies? They're not bothering anybody, and they're so pretty."

"Well, some people believe too many wild horses are running around these parts." Mike Woodson climbed over the fence so he could stand next to his daughter. "There isn't enough range, or grazing land, for the cattle *and* the Mustangs."

"Don't we have enough grazing land for all the animals?" Moxie Wyoming asked as she moved even closer to her father.

"There are ranchers who don't think we do," he answered. "They believe the Mustangs eat too much grass, and not enough is left for their cattle. They also say these horses damage the range and drink too much water in places that don't have enough."

"So what's gonna happen to the horses?" Moxie's voice got small and sad. "Will they die?" She blinked back tears.

"Well, some people break the law by rounding up Mustangs to sell and ship them out of the country. So..." He sighed, his eyes looking sad. "So, I'm afraid some of them will." Moxie's tears spilled down her cheeks.

He pulled his daughter close, and she dried her tears on his shirt. "I know it's hard, squirt. Another thing, the United States government has been rounding up a lot of Mustangs and moving them to pastures in the Midwest where there's more grass. Those roundups aren't against the law."

That sounded like a good possibility, Moxie thought, but her father didn't sound too cheerful. "Is it bad for the horses when th-th-the government rounds them up?" Moxie sniffled.

"To be honest, I'm not sure the government ones are so great either. Roundups stress and scare the horses and separate the foals from their mothers."

Moxie Wyoming put her hands on her hips and said, "I think wild Mustangs should stay free and go where they want!"

Misty, who had been napping during this conversation, woke up with a snort and a sneeze. She showed all her teeth like a huge smile, and both father and daughter burst into laughter.

"This old girl has been here about a week, and you two have had some time to get acquainted. Do you think you'd like to go out for a little ride?" Her father walked back to the pasture gate. "I've got to move some horses in Strawberry Meadow. Want to come?"

"You bet, Dad."

Just then, Pickle walked around the corner of the barn leading his black-and-white pony. "Hi, y'all. Want to come with me for a ride?" he asked Moxie. "Paint's saddle is big enough for both of us."

"Hi. I can't. I'm going to ride Misty and help Daddy check on some horses." Moxie Wyoming tried to sound very grownup.

"Misty?" Pickle asked, looking around. Then he pretended surprise. "Ohhhh, you mean that funny-looking horse standing there next to you?"

"Don't talk that way about Misty, Pickle Turner."

"Just kidding," Pickle said. "Don't be so bossy—"

"Okay, kids, settle down," Moxie's father said. "Pickle, would you and Paint like to join us?"

"Thanks, Mr. Woodson!" Pickle climbed up on Paint's saddle.

Within minutes, Moxie's dad had Misty saddled up. They all set off, and the ride over to Strawberry Meadow didn't take them very long.

Soon, the kids were helping move horses to another part of the ranch. Moxie definitely loved doing cowboy chores, and spending time with her dad and her best friend.

On their way back to the barn, Moxie Wyoming thought about how riding Misty was kind of confusing. She would give Misty a kick, and the mare would take off. Moxie liked the long, easy stride of her lope since it was slower than a gallop. But then after a while, Misty would start huffing and puffing and move in a bouncy, uncomfortable trot.

"What a slowpoke," Pickle teased as he rode alongside her on his pony.

"Pickle, don't make fun of Misty!" Moxie pulled back on the reins to slow down and give the mare a rest. "Sorry, Dad. I thought you said she used to be queen of the herd."

Before her father could answer, Misty came to a complete stop and folded her front legs down as though she were kneeling.

"Whoa!" Moxie hollered when Misty folded her back legs, too. "*Daaaaad!*" Her father jumped off his horse.

"Get off, get off!" Pickle yelled.

Moxie quickly pulled her feet out of the stirrups and pushed off the saddle. Misty plopped onto her side and started wriggling in the dust.

Her father came to Moxie's side. "You okay, squirt?"

"I'm fine." Moxie laughed and danced around Misty, who was still squirming on the ground. "It looks like Misty's got an itch, and she wants it scratched."

"I'm sure that wiggling around in the dust feels good to her," Moxie's father said. "I think maybe Misty's just trying to tell us that she's tired." Misty got up. "Kids, let's walk our horses home together."

"Sounds like a plan, Dad."

34

"You bet," Pickle said.

Just then Misty did the funny winking thing with her one eye, and this time both Moxie and Pickle saw her do it.

"Did you see that?" Pickle asked. "What's that thing Misty's doing with her eye?"

"Probably just a fly bothering her," Moxie answered, smiling at the ground.

"I dunno," Pickle said. "It kinda looked like a wink to me."

Moxie Wyoming had no doubt that Misty was winking at her, and she quickly winked back when Pickle wasn't looking.

"I've never seen a winking horse before," Pickle muttered. "That's just plain weird."

Moxie didn't think so. "You're weird, Pickle." She definitely wanted their winking thing to stay a secret, at least for now.

~~~~~

At dusk, Moxie Wyoming swept out the stall across from Misty's. It had been empty for a long time, and she had decided to claim it for herself. The stall had a creaky old cot, which she'd covered with blankets and brightly-colored pillows from the house.

Misty hung her head over her stall door to observe Moxie's decorating efforts.

"Dad said I could fix up this stall any way I want." Moxie wiped off a small, beat-up wooden desk. "And if you get lonely, you know, missing your horse friends—"

Misty gave a long, gentle whinny, like a sigh.

"—well, I can come stay here, and we can hang out."

The little mare batted her eyes.

Moxie smiled and unrolled an old hooked rug on the hard-dirt floor. She plugged in two lamps, a small one on the desk and a dented metal floor lamp near the cot.

Then Moxie pushed tacks into the walls to hang up her favorite posters and pictures of beautiful horses. One was a poster of a

Mustang herd grazing in a meadow. Moxie stood back, leaning against Misty's stall door to inspect her work.

"I wonder about those Mustangs in the Snowies," she said, looking at the poster. "I hope they're okay, Misty."

The small horse snorted.

Moxie Wyoming grabbed a large roll of paper, a handful of tacks, and a marker. "Somethin' else. Our ranch is almost four-hundred miles from where you used to live. Daddy showed me."

She marched into Misty's stall, unrolling the paper.

"So, this is for you to look at when you get homesick." She tacked up a map of the Gros Ventre Mountains east of Jackson and marked a huge *X* on one spot. Then she wrote *Darwin Ranch* in big letters next to the *X*.

Chapter Seven

Moxie Wyoming had finished her chores and skipped into the barn, pulling a carrot out of her back pocket. Misty delicately munched it from Moxie's hand.

Moxie looked around Misty's stall, pleased with her attempt to transform it into a magical space in just a couple of days. Half a dozen large Chinese moon lanterns now hung down from the ceiling. The paper moons had big smiles and turned in the gentle afternoon breeze.

Various portraits of Misty, signed by the artist, *Moxie Wyoming*, hung on the two side walls and around the map marking the Darwin Ranch. That back wall with the map also displayed another Moxie Wyoming original, a painted mural of an evergreen forest in the mountains.

Strands of twinkling colored lights and other ones with horse and cowboy hat lights draped the top of the walls near the ceiling. The final touch was Misty's water bucket, now covered with glitter and tied with a huge red bow.

"If I were a horse, I'd like living here." Moxie continued looking around. "You like it, girl?"

Misty took her right front leg and pounded her hoof twice. Moxie watched her hoof and looked up in surprise. She remembered the other day when Misty had thumped the ground twice for a horse treat when she was in the paddock.

"Is that a *yes*?"

The mare grabbed Moxie's shirt sleeve with her teeth and again pounded her hoof twice.

"Hey! I get it. Wow! Okay. Let's see, how would you say *no*?" Moxie wondered. "Hmmm. Let me think of a question that I'm positive you would say *no* to." She hesitated for only a moment. "Do you like fire?" This time Misty took her left front leg and thumped hard on the ground *one* time.

Moxie smiled. "Okay. Here's another one. Are you a foal, you know, a baby horse?" The little mare again thumped her left leg on the ground once.

Moxie looked from the hoof into Misty's eyes. "So that's how you say *no*. One thump with the left hoof for *no* and two thumps with the right hoof to say *yes*?"

Misty pounded twice with her right front leg.

"This is amazing. I've never *really* talked to a horse before. I mean, I've never had one talk back to me. This is so cool! Is this some kind of magic?"

Misty whinnied softly, batting her eyes as she answered.

Moxie Wyoming grinned from ear to ear. "And you wink, too. That was you winking, wasn't it, when you do that thing with your eye?"

Misty thumped twice with her front right leg and winked to give her answer a little something extra.

Moxie noticed the mare's eyelashes were looking rather sparse. *Oh well,* she thought, as she rubbed Misty's forehead. *She's got those skimpy lashes because she's old, like over thirty. Well, she may be old, but she can talk to me, and that's just plain amazing!*

Beaming, Moxie Wyoming kicked up her heels on her way out of the little horse's stall and sang, "I can talk to Misty, Misty can talk to me-ee." *Well, not really talk-talk, but I know what my horse means,* she thought.

Moxie skipped over to her own stall where she'd also applied her decorating skills. She twirled, surveying the results of her work. She had painted the desk a glossy red. Art supplies for an almost-finished *Moxie Wyoming* painting covered the top of the desk.

Dangling chimes draped the beat-up floor lamp that now stood next to a worn-out, overstuffed chair covered in colorful Native American blankets. A small pine bookcase leaned against the wall by the big chair. Horse novels filled its shelves, and horse statues, arranged lovingly, stood in clusters across the top of the bookcase.

"Moxie Wyoming, you in there?" Willie Turner's voice called from outside the barn.

"Yes, Mr. Turner," Moxie answered.

She looked at the rest of the horse statues filling a pine shelf on the wall over the cot. This stall also had twinkling lights draped over all the walls. Curtains made from old flannel cowgirl sheets hung on the window.

"Hey, Mr. Turner," she hollered. "Thanks for helping me hang these curtains and all these lights and lanterns. Misty thanks you, too. I think she likes her stall a lot."

Pickle's dad stood next to the stall door and laughed. "How many times do I have to remind you that when you say *Mr. Turner*, I think you mean my dad. You know you're supposed to call me Willie."

He held a big box wrapped in brown paper and tied with heavy string. "Anyway, UPS just delivered this, and it's for you." He put the box on the cot.

"Who's it from?" Moxie asked.

"Don't know," he said. "I guess you'd better open it."

"Thanks, Willie," Moxie called after him, as he walked out. "Please say hi to Pickle!"

Moxie Wyoming and Misty gazed at the box, which seemed to glow slightly. *Maybe it's just from the twinkle lights shining on it,* she thought.

Searching for scissors, Moxie glanced at her desk. By the time she looked back at the cot, the package had stopped glowing. Misty still stared at it.

"There sure are some funny-weird things going on today, Misty." Moxie cut the brown paper. "The return address is smudged, I can't read it...hmmm."

Moxie pulled off the paper, opened the flaps of the box, and pushed aside white tissue paper. When she saw what was inside, she caught her breath.

Moxie Wyoming carefully lifted out a pair of old, but beautiful, two-toned, pink leather cowgirl boots with dark-pink stitching in the shape of flowers. A silver star decorated the center of each flower.

"Oh, Misty, look!" She kicked off her sneakers as the mare continued peering from her stall door and watched her mistress slowly slip her feet into the boots.

Testing the fit of her new boots, Moxie walked across the hooked rug. "They feel so soft, like my fuzzy slippers!" She admired them every which way on her feet. "I wonder who sent them?"

Moxie rummaged around in the box and pulled out a small brown leather pouch with beautiful turquoise and coral beading. "Hey, what's this?" She opened it.

Moxie uncoiled a gold chain with a gold whistle hanging on it. "Cool!" She put the chain around her neck and tooted softly on the whistle. Misty immediately kicked once loudly on the stall door with her left leg.

Startled, Moxie dropped the whistle from her mouth. "Was that a *do-not-whistle* kick?"

Misty pounded the ground twice with her right leg.

"Hmmm. So you *don't* want me to blow it?"

Misty again pounded twice.

"That must mean you know something about this whistle."

Misty pounded *yes* once more.

"Is it...magic?" Moxie Wyoming whispered, and Misty answered with two stomps.

"So what kind of magic exactly?" Moxie examined the whistle more closely, tapping it with her fingernail. "It looks like a regular whistle."

Misty snorted a couple of times, as if saying, *Don't kid yourself.*

"So I have to wait to find out more?" Moxie asked, and Misty pounded *yes.*

Moxie looked inside the box again, and this time she pulled out a card.

Dear Moxie Wyoming,

Here's a present for you to go along with your new horse! The boots and the whistle belonged to your Granny Rose, so take good care of them. You'll discover they are one of a kind, and Misty is, too!

Lots of love,

Grandpops

Moxie turned her attention back to the boots. She stretched her legs and toes so she could get a better look. Then she jumped up and dashed out.

Once inside the house, Moxie stood on her tippy-toes to examine the painting of Granny Rose sitting on her pretty black horse. She looked closely at her great-grandmother's feet and saw she was wearing a pair of pink boots. Moxie looked at the pink boots on her own feet and knew they were the very same pair.

Moxie Wyoming pulled a chair over to the painting and climbed up to get an even better look. She thought she saw the hint of a gold chain hanging around her great-grandmother's neck. She felt the gold chain around her own neck, jumped down from the chair, and rushed into her room.

Chapter Eight

Moxie Wyoming sashayed back into the barn. "How do I look, girl?" she asked as she twirled her way up to Misty's stall. The mare opened her eyes from yet another nap.

"Hey, Misty, check me out!" If Granny Rose always wore pink when she rode, then Moxie would, too. She modeled a completely pink riding outfit—a pink rain slicker, pink riding tights, and the pink cowgirl boots. Misty snorted her approval.

"We should go for a ride so I can try out my new boots. What do you think?" Moxie twirled around again, and Misty neighed *yes* and stomped her right hoof twice.

Outside, Moxie saddled up her elderly friend and climbed on board. The two headed across a scrubby field in the direction of the foothills below the Snowies. They walked slowly and enjoyed a perfect blue-sky afternoon.

As Moxie watched large brown grasshoppers jump around the brush, she gave Misty a gentle kick with her new boots. The old mare trotted and then moved into her familiar lope.

But this time, a funny thing happened. Instead of huffing and puffing and slowing down as she usually did, Misty turned frisky, throwing her head around and neighing loudly. Moxie's expression changed from surprise to interest as Misty picked up her pace.

She also noticed that the gray flecks all over Misty's body were disappearing, and her black coat had become shinier and smoother.

"What's happening to you? Where did all your gray go?" Moxie reached down to touch and stroke the hair on the horse's neck. "It can't just go away, can it? What's going on here?"

Moxie Wyoming spotted a coyote fifty yards away, near the bank of a stream. "Hey! Let's take a look." The creature was larger than a fox, but smaller than a wolf.

She gave Misty another slight kick with her pink cowgirl boots. "Let's go!"

Misty loped faster and faster. The coyote didn't move, but watched them with pale, glowing eyes. Moxie noticed a barbed wire fence right behind the animal, as her horse picked up more speed. Moxie cried out, "Whoa! Stop! Whoa!"

Before they could smash into the fence, Misty jumped and sailed over it as if she were a young colt instead of an old horse. Instead of landing near the bank of the stream, she continued lifting higher and higher.

"*Yikes*, Misty!" Moxie shrieked. She looked around her. They were flying! "*Ooohhh, nooooo!*" With her one hand locked around the horn of the saddle and gripping the reins, the other clutched a huge chunk of Misty's mane. As they soared well above the ground, everything down there became very small. The coyote now looked about the size of a mouse!

Suddenly, the wind knocked Misty back, and they dropped thirty feet. Moxie Wyoming screamed the entire way down, knowing they were going to crash. But Misty threw her head up, flicked her tail, and recovered instantly to once again lift them both into the air.

The rollercoaster ride continued, and after three more bumpy ups-and-downs of Misty trying out her flying skills with a rider on board, Moxie's face turned a funny shade of green. "Misty, *pleeease* can we land? My tummy's doing tumble-saults." She hung over Misty's neck like a limp noodle.

Misty threw out all four of her legs, which started horse and rider twirling and floating light as feathers down to the ground in a perfect helicopter landing. Moxie barely felt them touch down.

They stood quietly, the girl not quite believing what had just happened. Finally, she spoke in a shaky voice. "Am I dreaming?"

The little mare pounded *no* with her left foot. "So I'm not going to wake up?"

The hoof pounded *no* again.

"Misty, is this the first time you've done this, uh, flying thing?"

The mare answered *no* a third time.

"Wow!" Moxie looked at her horse curiously. "You mean you've been flying around for a long time?"

Misty snorted and pounded *yes.*

"Has anybody ever seen you fly, besides me, I mean?"

Misty looked up at the sky.

"Okay, I'm not sure what that means." Moxie paused. "Has anybody else ever flown...with you?"

The mare stomped *yes.*

Moxie's face filled with surprise and curiosity. "I wonder who else got to fly with you?"

The horse nickered softly.

Moxie leaned over Misty's neck. "I guess you're a little out of practice carrying a rider while you fly, maybe because you've been at the Darwin Ranch a long time," Moxie said. "That's why it felt so bumpy, you know, all up and down?"

Misty pounded *yes* again.

Then Moxie Wyoming leaned over smiling, laid her head along Misty's neck, and reached down both sides with her arms to give the mare a huge hug. "You're amazing, Misty."

As they walked back to the barn, Moxie noticed that Misty slowed down and huffed and puffed a bit. She stopped acting frisky, and gray hairs once again flecked her coat.

"Hey, what's going on with you?" Sadly, Moxie realized that Misty was back to her *old* self.

She leaned over a second time, reaching her arms down both sides of Misty's gray-flecked neck, and gave her another huge hug. "I love you both ways—the other way and this way, too," she whispered.

~~~~~

As Moxie and Misty walked up to the barn, Pickle waved from the corral fence, his dusty ATV parked nearby. The boy chewed on a piece of straw. "Hey, where have you been? We haven't played detectives or gone riding in a while—"

"Pickle, it's only been a few days." Moxie gestured toward Misty. "I've been very busy."

"Me, too," he grumbled. "So how's Misty?"

"Pretty good." Moxie smiled. "She's new—"

"She doesn't look very *new* to me!" Pickle snickered.

"Not funny, Pickle Turner," Moxie shot back, climbing down from the saddle. "You don't know anything about her."

"Well, one thing I do know, Moxie Wyoming. Your horse may be kind of cute, but you can't ride her in barrel races." Pickle jumped off the fence. "She's too old!"

"Actually, Misty's very special!" Moxie insisted.

"Yeah, right." Pickle rolled his eyes. "Well, I hope you aren't busy forever, Moxie Wyoming." He hopped on the ATV and drove off, leaving Moxie and Misty sneezing in a cloud of dust.

Chapter Nine

During the next week, Moxie Wyoming rode Misty daily. The two practiced the flying part in secret. Whenever Moxie said, "Let's go," it was the start of a new adventure!

The girl and the mare had ironed out a lot of the bumps. Since that first ride, Moxie hadn't turned green too often, just different shades of purple or blue. She quickly learned not to practice flying right after lunch on a full stomach.

But she did like to imagine the places that Misty might take her, places that she and her mom had read about together or had watched on TV—the Serengeti National Park in Africa to see the great migrations of wildebeests and zebras; Florida to watch the dolphins and visit the Ringling Brothers' clown school (*How cool*, Moxie thought, *to go to clown class instead of math*); the South Pole to catch sight of penguins and check out the monster icebergs; and Hollywood to see where the old TV shows were made about the famous collie, Lassie, and the cowboy, Roy Rogers, with his trusted horse, Trigger.

At the moment, Moxie was daydreaming about cuddly kangaroo babies in Australia. "Whew! The sun's really hot," She and Misty scuffed along a dusty trail at the far corner of the ranch. "Let's ride where it's cool."

Gathering up Misty's reins, Moxie looked up at the Snowy Range. "Like over there, up in the mountains, Misty. I bet it's cooler in the shade of all those trees." She gently kicked with her pink cowgirl boots.

Turning frisky, Misty threw her head around, neighed, and launched into a smooth lope. Her coat lost its gray flecks and became shiny and pure black.

Moxie Wyoming rode Misty confidently, and at just the right moment, she said, "Let's go." The mare pushed off her back legs, and they sailed effortlessly into the sky.

The two friends flew over the neighboring ranches where the buildings now looked like dollhouses. A majestic eagle soared next to them. He was so close Moxie could almost reach out and fluff his feathers. The eagle cut to the right and looped around Moxie and Misty.

"Hey, Mr. Eagle, looking good! Mind if we join you up here?!" Moxie laughed as the powerful bird dove down and away like a plane.

The mare and her rider flew over the foothills and canyons of the Snowies, and Moxie enjoyed the alpine scenery of rocky cliffs and evergreen trees. As they sailed over one canyon, Moxie noticed a flash of movement.

"Go back, Misty! There's something down there," she said with urgency. "It ran into the cover. Go back!"

Misty banked to the side and circled back, dropping down. They glided within the walls of the canyon at fifty feet above the ground to get a closer look.

"There!" Moxie cried out, as she and Misty sailed above a herd of horses led by a palomino-colored stallion coming out of the woods into the open. Misty slowed her speed to stay a little behind the herd.

"Those have got to be the wild Mustangs that Willie's friend saw up here," Moxie said. "There must be almost twenty horses, and look! Some mares with their foals! They're so cute!"

The Mustang herd slowed down as it came to a pond, and the horses spread out for a drink. The girl and her horse landed in a clearing on the other side of some trees. They moved quietly into the trees, hidden, watching the Mustangs.

Suddenly the herd became restless and stirred nervously. The stallion reared and neighed loudly. A dark brown mare with a black mane and tail neighed, too, and took off to gallop higher into the mountains. The rest of the Mustangs quickly followed, and the stallion brought up the rear, the sun shining off his pale yellow body.

Moxie and Misty didn't budge. "That's what Pickle and I read in that book, Misty. That was the lead mare taking the herd up the mountain. And the stallion was at the back to protect them from danger." She looked around nervously. "Hmmm. What kind of danger?"

Just then Moxie saw a couple of herding dogs pop out on the trail below. Still concealed by the trees, she watched as two riders in well-worn cowboy hats came up behind the barking mutts. Moxie felt goose bumps on her arms. The men rode up to the pond to study the tracks near the water.

A crusty voice came out from under a moss-colored cowboy hat and said, "Looks like that herd was here."

Moxie couldn't see his face, and she wasn't sure she recognized the voice.

"Finally, after all that hunting around, we found the right canyon," he said. She wondered if it was those Jenkins men from the rodeo and secret corral.

"We gotta get a helicopter and round them up," the other cowboy—wait a minute—uh, cowgirl said, as her black ponytail swung into view from underneath her dark, reddish-brown hat. "Nobody'll miss them, and a lot of other ranchers b-b-besides us will be happy to see them go."

Moxie realized she was wrong. It wasn't those two creepy brothers. It was the man and young woman she had seen loading the

51

truck next to her dad's at the feed store, the truck that said *Curly T Cattle Ranch* on its side.

"Forget the helicopter, Jamie. It'll attract too much attention," the man barked. "Listen to your old man for a change."

Jamie's posture wilted in the saddle as the cowboy took off his hat and wiped his brow. Moxie noticed the skin on his face was as leathery as his voice was gravelly.

"I betcha we can track them and find out where those Mustangs bed down," he said.

Still out of sight, Moxie listened with alarm, her heart pounding in her chest. Misty's ears went flat and back along her head. *Sounds like he's the father and that's his daughter*, Moxie thought. Even so, she knew their plans for the Mustangs couldn't be good after what she had heard them say at the feed store.

Misty's ears stayed flat against her head, and she snorted in disgust.

The two riders whipped around at the sound and peered into the thicket. "Hey, Dad!" Jamie pointed toward the trees. "Do you think they went over th-there, instead of further up the mountain? It looks l-l-like the tracks go up, but—"

"Only one way to find out." The man kicked his horse to take off, and he and his daughter rode in Moxie's direction.

But Misty was ready for them and took off at a faster clip. As soon and she and Moxie cleared the woods, Moxie said, "Let's go!" The horse then pushed off her back legs.

Moxie Wyoming and Misty were immediately airborne and high enough to circle around. They watched the two riders dash about below, looking for the horses.

Misty seemed to sense something going on. Moxie felt a quiver go through her when the little horse snorted once, and her ears twitched back and forth quickly. Just then, Jamie and her father looked up at the sky; Moxie froze and held her breath as she clung to her saddle.

But the two on the ground didn't appear to see the horse and girl flying around above them. The riders finally gave up and continued up the mountain, but the Mustang herd was long gone by then.

"Misty, how come they didn't see us?" Moxie asked. "What did you do? Did you make us invisible up here flying around?"

Misty snorted *yes* twice, since she couldn't stomp at that moment.

Moxie felt another quiver and Misty twitched her ears again. "Are we still invisible?"

Misty snorted *no*.

"This is like being in a comic book with super heroes!" Moxie said, and she and her mare flew home.

Finally, they could see Moose Creek Ranch and began their descent.

"Jamie wants to get a helicopter to round up those beautiful horses. A helicopter buzzing around would be scary for the horses. Right, Misty?"

The little mare snorted twice in agreement.

Moxie Wyoming and Misty landed in a pasture and walked in the direction of the barn. "With the Jenkins brothers and now that man and his daughter from the Curly T ranch against them, the Mustangs need more friends on their side. And that's you and me, Misty."

The small horse snorted and did a mini-kick with her back legs to show she agreed.

Chapter Ten

"*Mo-om*, where are my pink boots?" Moxie Wyoming hollered, as she rummaged through her closet several days later. "I can't find them, and I want to ride." Shoes, slippers, and boots came flying out one after the other from her closet. Bunker, watching intently, ducked and barked every time a shoe or slipper zoomed by.

"Bunker! Settle down!" Moxie's mother called from the ranch office. "I took the boots to the cobbler, kiddo, to get the heels fixed. They looked kind of worn down, but wasn't that nice of Grandpops to send them to you?"

"Yes, Mom. They're my very favorite. I *have* to wear them to ride."

"Granny Rose's boots will be back in a couple of days," Moxie's mother said. "Wear your brown boots until then."

"Oh, Mom, you totally *don't* get it."

~~~~~

So there she was in her pink slicker and pink riding tights, but in the—ugh!—old brown cowgirl boots, saddling up Misty, who stared at the boots. "I know, I know. These definitely don't go with my outfit."

Moxie walked Misty through the back pasture and climbed on board. "These boots don't feel as comfy as the pink ones either..." She gave Misty a little kick and the horse moved into an easy lope.

Once they were some distance from the house, Moxie asked, "Well, girl, how 'bout it? Want to try to find those Mustangs again?"

Misty threw up her head and neighed several times as she trotted, picking up some speed. Moxie took hold of Misty's mane, gave her a confident kick, and said, "Let's go!"

Misty continued loping. Again, Moxie said, "Let's go!" Nothing happened. She noticed that Misty was huffing and puffing, and the gray remained in her coat.

One more time. "Let's go!" Nothing. Misty and Moxie slowed down and came to a stop so that the horse's breathing could settle down.

"What's the matter? Don't feel like flying today?"

Misty's hoof pounded *yes* as her breathing returned to normal.

Moxie leaned over and hugged Misty around her neck. "It's okay, girl."

Misty snorted her disappointment.

"I wonder why it's not working..."

Moxie glanced down at her dull brown boots and her face lit up. "It's the boots!"

Misty whinnied.

"Do I need the pink boots when we want to fly?"

Misty pounded the ground twice with her right leg to say *yes*.

"Hmmm, those boots have some powerful magic!" Moxie Wyoming said. Misty neighed loudly, and Moxie giggled.

Even though the Snowies didn't look that far away, Moxie decided to steer Misty back toward the ranch. As the mare shuffled along a rocky trail on the side of a scrubby hill, Moxie stared down at the grasshoppers jumping around Misty's legs and zoned out.

"Hey you, kid!" a gruff voice up ahead hollered out from under a brown cowboy hat, startling Moxie and Misty. Moxie recognized the voice right away. It was Jeb Jenkins from the rodeo. She shivered as she caught a glimpse of his blotchy face and a scar running down one of his cheeks. She looked around, now fully alert, wondering where his partner was or if he was riding alone.

Jeb raised his fingers to his mouth and whistled loudly. To Moxie's horror, another cowboy, the one with the charcoal-gray hat, rode out from behind several huge boulders uphill.

"Yeah, what's up?" the second cowboy asked, as he walked his horse down to the trail. When he pushed up his hat and caught sight of Moxie, she glimpsed his crooked nose. "Well, Jeb, lookie what we have here," he snickered.

"Hey, Frank, isn't that one of those kids we saw? The ones who was spyin', uh, I mean, checkin' out the corral we were buildin'?" Jeb asked. "It's a little hard to tell though, 'cause those kids had helmets. Do you think she's one of 'em?"

"Could be. What should we do about it?" Frank asked in a loud voice while looking straight at Moxie. "Do you think we should have a talk with her about what we're doin'...you know, our plan to find nice horses, wild ones, for orphan kids and keep 'em in the corral until we tame—"

"You stay away from from Misty and me!" Moxie Wyoming interrupted, using her loudest voice.

Moxie grew more and more nervous as the two men continued to walk their horses slowly in her direction. They blocked her path home, and she wondered if she and Misty should turn around and gallop away.

But there were two of them, and she wasn't wearing the pink boots. If they came after her, they'd catch her for sure.

All of a sudden, Moxie remembered the gold chain hanging around her neck and slowly pulled it out from her shirt. She fingered the whistle on the end, while Misty backed up, throwing her head from side to side and snorting.

Jeb spit on the ground. *Ew, gross,* Moxie thought, settling her mare and grasping the whistle. Those guys were getting closer; she hoped they couldn't hear her teeth chattering from fear.

Leaning down, Moxie whispered to Misty, "Should I blow it?"

Misty tapped the ground with her right hoof twice.

Moxie blew into the magic whistle with all her might until she couldn't exhale anymore. The cowboys stopped, surprised, but then started laughing. Moxie blew the whistle again. It screeched loudly, and the men plugged their ears with their fingers.

"Whew, that's loud," Frank said. "If I didn't know better, I'd think she's tryin' to scare us."

"Oh, I think I'm gettin' scared." Jeb smirked.

But Moxie was the one who was terrified. Terrified, tired, and winded. Still, she blew the whistle a third time.

"Are you scared now, Jeb?"

"Oh, *reeeal* scared, Frank. Listen here, little lady. No need to—"

Misty neighed loudly as Moxie turned to make a getaway on the rocky path. Hugging tightly to Misty, she felt her heart thump in her chest as she and her horse pounded down the trail. Moxie didn't dare look back, but she could hear the brothers riding in her direction on the bumpy path.

"Wait," Frank called out. "We just want to tell you about the orphan kids! You might wanna help us—"

A loud roar thundered down from the side of the hill. Startled, the three of them stopped and looked up. A ferocious brown bear, at least ten feet tall, was up on its hind legs; it growled again.

"Frank, isn't that a grizzly?" Jeb's voice was shaky, and his horse nervously danced on the trail. "Whoa, boy."

"Yep. Don't look him in the eye, and back up slowly," Frank said. "We need to get outta here."

The animal raced down the hill toward Frank and Jeb. Between its shoulders, Moxie could see the distinctive grizzly bear hump that her dad had shown her in photographs. She also noticed that one of its ears had a notch in it, like a tear from an old battle. The grizzly chased the two men, who galloped a speedy retreat.

Moxie's mouth hung open in surprise, and her eyes went wide. "Holy-moly...is that what's supposed to happen?" she asked Misty.

Misty pounded *yes*, and Moxie smiled, looking at the gold whistle. "That's better than having a bodyguard. Wouldn't it be cool to take him to school?"

Misty snorted a distinctive *no*.

"It was just a thought. Geez..." Moxie tucked the whistle safely inside her shirt, and they continued home. "Well, one thing we know is that the Jenkins brothers want to put horses in that secret corral. And I don't think those horses are for orphan kids."

As Misty walked along the path to the ranch, Moxie thought more about the secret corral.

"Where will they get horses to put in that corral?" she wondered.

Moxie suddenly flashed on the palomino stallion, the chestnut lead mare, and the Mustang herd she had seen in the Snowies, and put two and two together. "Wild horses! That's it! They want to round up Mustangs." Moxie stared down at her stirrups and wiggled her toes in the brown boots.

"Let's see. When Pickle and I saw them at the rodeo, those guys talked about a roundup and making money. Probably they want to sell the Mustangs. And like Daddy said, they'll break the law by selling them to people who will send the horses away."

Moxie was eager to get back since Pickle was coming over. She hoped Pickle wasn't still a grouch about all the time she was spending with Misty because she had important detective news to tell him.

Moxie wanted Pickle to know that she had figured out what the Jenkins guys were up to. She also wanted to tell Pickle about the folks from the Curly T Cattle Ranch, and that the girl, Jamie, wanted to round up the Mustangs with a helicopter.

Boy, that would *really* scare the horses.

Moxie even wondered if Jamie and her father were working together with those brothers on the same roundup. Maybe if she and Pickle did more detective work, they could figure it out.

Moxie sighed, and wished she could share with her best friend what had just happened with the gold whistle and grizzly bear. But Pickle would never believe it in a million years. Moxie Wyoming hardly believed it herself.

Chapter Eleven

It was that time of year again—Laramie Jubilee Days, in honor of Wyoming's birthday. It had become a state in 1890, and Moxie and Pickle were having fun at the week-long anniversary celebration.

Moxie Wyoming was in her best cowgirl outfit, a short denim skirt with suede fringe and a rhinestone-studded pink vest over a blue shirt. The vest had been a special Christmas present from her grandfather. It looked perfect with Granny Rose's newly repaired pink leather boots.

Pickle looked very Western, too, in his denim jacket with cactus designs. Both kids wore straw cowboy hats that Moxie's dad had bought them before he'd signed up for the ranch rodeo competition. They had cheered and waved their hats when his team came in first in trailer loading.

As they walked along, Moxie and Pickle laughed each time they tipped their hats at each other. They stopped at a stand where a grizzled old cowboy was bent over, scooping up snow cones.

"Well, well, a couple of real young-uns. What can I getcha?" he asked, his bright blue eyes crinkling.

"Two snow cones, please." Moxie pulled money out of her pocket. "My treat, Pickle. Mom gave me money for both of us."

The gray-bearded man scooped the cherry-colored ice into two paper cones. "Are you havin' fun at Jubilee Days?"

"Yes, sir," the kids answered in unison. Moxie noticed that even though the old cowpoke was clean and tidy, his clothes and boots were old and kind of worn out.

"Have you been coming here a long time, mister?" she asked, as she noticed the big shiny silver buckle on his belt.

"Oh, 'bout sixty years," he chuckled. "Here you go." Moxie and Pickle tried hard not to stare at his gnarly knuckles and shaky hands as he gave them the paper cones. They thanked him, and then rushed across the road to a bench where they licked the icy snow cones.

Moxie and Pickle stiffened when they saw the Jenkins brothers saunter up to the stand and order. It had only been a few days since Moxie watched the grizzly bear chase the two cowboys. She was surprised to see them here at Jubilee Days.

Hoping to stay unnoticed, she and Pickle pushed their hats down to cover more of their faces and didn't say a word. But the cowboys were too busy making fun of the old man to notice the children.

Jeb suddenly reached toward the elderly cowpoke as if to tug his beard, causing the fellow to step back and nervously drop one of the cones on the ground.

"Useless old man," Frank muttered. They threw their money on the ground and walked away, cackling at him.

As the man slowly stooped over to pick up the coins, Moxie thought back to the day Misty had first arrived at Moose Creek Ranch. She remembered feeling so disappointed when she had thought Misty was an old, broken-down nag. Now, of course, she knew better.

"They are so mean," she muttered under her breath. "He's *not* just some useless old man!"

"What?" Pickle asked.

"That old guy," Moxie said. "Didn't you hear them make fun of him?"

"Yeah," Pickle answered.

"Well, did you see that big belt buckle the snow cone man's got? It's like the ones hanging on the wall at home. You know, from when my dad competed in rodeos."

"Somebody probably gave it to him." Pickle slurped the last of his cone. "He's really old, Moxie."

"You don't know that. Maybe a long, long, long time ago, he was a rodeo champion and won that buckle. You know, before he sold snow cones," she said.

"Him? No way," Pickle said.

Moxie thought of her Misty, who looked old to the rest of the world. "You never know. Maybe he used to be like my dad and could do lots of stuff."

The kids threw away their empty paper cones, and Moxie pulled Pickle back over to the snow cone stand. "Are you okay, mister?" she asked. The old cowboy looked at them, confused, with sad eyes, like maybe he expected more trouble.

"We saw those two guys bothering you," Moxie said.

"And they were so mean," Pickle piped up.

"Should we find the sheriff? You know, to report them?"

The old man's expression softened. "No, no. I'm fine. Thank you for being a nice to an old cowpoke like me." His blue eyes twinkled again. "You kids be on your way and have a good time here at Jubilee Days. Thanks for askin' though."

"You're welcome, mister," Moxie said.

"Bye!" Pickle added. They waved at the old man and continued walking around the area surrounding the rodeo arena. Moxie wondered if the old man had known her Granny Rose from her rodeo days.

"Look!" Pickle said, his eyes the size of saucers.

"What?" Moxie asked.

Pickle pointed across the road at a tall, brown-haired cowgirl, coming from the Ferris wheel. "That's Mary Lou Hendricks!"

"Yeah?" Moxie wasn't impressed. "So?"

"My mom read about her and showed me her picture. Mom says she's very important, because she's Queen of Jubilee Days, so she's like a V.I.P., you know, very important person—"

"I know what a V.I.P. is, Pickle," she said, looking at the cowgirl in the red shirt and tan leather vest edged in red. Her matching tan leather chaps were fringed with the same red, and *Miss Laramie Jubilee Days* was embroidered in red down the right leg. Moxie gawked at the shiny, ruby-red cowgirl boots peeking out from the bottom of the tan chaps.

"She's so pretty." Pickle, still staring, moon-eyed, pulled Moxie across the road to get a closer look.

But Miss Laramie Jubilee Days spotted them first. "My, my! Don't you two look adorable!" Mary Lou said, smiling.

Pickle grinned from ear to ear. Moxie stood mesmerized by the sparkly tiara attached to the young woman's red cowboy hat. Finally, the first words out of Moxie's mouth were, "Are those real diamonds?"

Mary Lou pointed at her tiara and laughed. "These? No, they're rhinestones. You know, pretend-diamonds." She reached out to shake their hands. "Hi, I'm Mary Lou Hendricks."

Moxie grabbed Mary Lou's hand and pumped it hard, maybe a little too hard. "I'm Moxie Wyoming Woodson, and this is my best friend, Pickle Turner." Before Pickle could shake Mary Lou's hand, Moxie jumped in with another question. "Is it hard being *Miss Laramie Jubilee Days*?"

"Well, it can be busy, but I love it," Mary Lou said. "I always dreamed of being a rodeo queen, so I get to represent the Laramie rodeo all year long during my reign."

"How did you get picked to be queen?" Pickle blurted out. "Is it tough? Do you have to do lots of rodeo stuff?"

Mary Lou smiled. "I started out by coming up through the princess program. Moxie, maybe you'd like to sign up."

Moxie scrunched her face with doubt. "So what do you do when you're not a rodeo queen?"

Mary Lou burst into laughter, and the kids joined in. "So many questions, you two. I'm training to work as a sheriff's deputy right here in Laramie."

Moxie and Pickle's eyes grew huge. "*You're* going to arrest people?" Moxie asked.

"You're too pretty to arrest people," Pickle said, and then clapped a hand over his mouth.

"I don't wear all this make-up and these fancy clothes when I'm working my other job," Mary Lou said. "My hair's in a ponytail, and I wear a uniform—"

"Do you have a favorite kind of horse?" Moxie Wyoming interrupted. "Like...um...what do you think of wild Mustangs?"

"I love all horses, so of course I love Mustangs," Mary Lou said, and Moxie's face lit up.

Mary Lou continued, "Mustangs are extra special. When people see a Mustang, they think of the American West. But some bad people are rounding up wild horses to ship them out of the country illegally, and that's wrong." The kids hung on every word Mary Lou said, and she smiled at them. "Why do you ask about wild horses?"

"Oh, nothing. Just curious," Moxie stammered, glancing at the ground. "If it's okay...I mean, would you mind...uh, could I have your phone number, please?"

Curious, Mary Lou looked at her for a moment, then pulled out a card and wrote her number on the back. "This is my private cell phone number. You call me if you ever need help or want to tell me something, all right?" She tipped her hat at the kids. "I have to be on my way, but I really enjoyed our conversation."

"Thank you." Moxie smiled as Mary Lou walked off. "Bye." She looked at the card with the phone number and tucked it into her vest pocket.

Chapter Twelve

"Where have you two been?" Mike Woodson asked his daughter, when Moxie and Pickle walked up to him. Smiling, he added, "We were getting ready to send out a posse."

"Daddy, you'll never believe it!" Moxie exclaimed. "We just met—"

"Miss Laramie Jubilee Days," Pickle piped up. "And she's cool. Her name is Mary Lou Hendricks."

"And, Dad, we had a conversation with her," Moxie said with self-importance. "That's why it took us so long."

"Well, do you think you're ready to pack it in?" Jane Woodson put one arm around her daughter and the other around Pickle. "You've been running around since Jubilee Days opened up this morning. You must be exhausted—"

"Nooooo, Mom. Pleeeease," Moxie begged.

"Excuse me, excuse me." Pickle raised a hand as if he were still in school. "Moxie and I were wondering if we could stay for the big parade?"

"Please, please, please," Moxie continued pleading. "And the fireworks, too—" She halted mid-sentence as she looked at a gazebo across the road and saw Officer Clem Brown talking with the Curly T Cattle Ranch people.

The conversation looked like an important one, because they stood close to each other as if they didn't want anybody else to hear what they were saying.

"Mom, Dad, look over there. Who is that?" Moxie Wyoming quickly nudged Pickle.

They all turned at the same time to see. The three by the gazebo noticed, stopped talking, and waved. Moxie's parents waved back.

"That's Officer Brown from the highway patrol," her dad said.

"Right, but who are those other two people he's talking to?" Moxie asked.

"That's Sam Bingham and his daughter, Jamie," Moxie's dad said. "They own the Curly T Cattle Ranch in Centennial Valley, like us. But they're at the other end of the valley, pretty far away from Moose Creek Ranch. Anyway, you don't see much of them around since Sam's wife, Trish, died a few years back."

"It hasn't been easy for Jamie either. She's very young, only nineteen or twenty," Moxie's mother said. "Sam always wanted a son to run the ranch, and he's tough on Jamie. Why do you ask, Moxie—"

A ring tone interrupted their conversation. Her mom pulled a cell phone out of her pocket. "Hello, Willie. Everything okay?" She listened, and her face went white. Pickle seemed to notice, and his brows scrunched.

"When did this happen?" Moxie's mother continued listening while looking at her husband with concern.

"Are my mom and dad okay?" Pickle spoke up, worried.

"Your parents are fine," Jane Woodson said, covering the phone, then turning back to the caller.

"We'll leave right away," she said into the phone, looking for a moment at Moxie. "We'll be home in less than an hour."

"What?" Moxie asked, once her mother hung up.

"Now, kids, let's go over there and sit down," Moxie's mom said. "I've got something important to tell you." She and Moxie's dad walked the girls toward a bench.

Moxie and Pickle looked at her with growing alarm. "What's going on?"

"Remember when your dad went off to fix that spot where the fence was down, the one that Officer Brown called him about?"

"Yeah, but Dad fixed it, right?" She and Pickle sat down on the bench.

"Yes, honey, he fixed it," Moxie's mother said. "But it turns out we might have another place where the fence is down. Most of the horses were already in the barn, but a few others still got through." She kneeled in front of Moxie. "Four of the horses were hurt."

Pickle jumped in. "How? Did a car hit them?"

"We don't know—"

Moxie grabbed Pickle's arm. "Which horses, Mom?"

"A driver found them on the road and called the highway patrol, who called Willie. He's on his way there right now to find out more."

"Which horses, Mom?" Moxie's voice grew shaky.

"The driver described them as two medium-sized chestnut horses—"

Pickle interrupted, "Guyetta and Mozart!"

"Who else, Mom?" Moxie's eyes blinked back tears.

"Two black horses..." Mrs. Woodson paused, looking at her husband, who put his arm around Moxie.

"One of them was small and gray-flecked," she finished. "Willie thinks it might have been Misty."

Moxie Wyoming took in a sharp breath and started to cry as her dad folded her into his arms.

She cried all the way home in the truck, thinking about Misty, hoping her elderly mare would be okay.

~~~~~

"Oh, good," Moxie's father said, as the truck pulled into the ranch. "Dr. Johnson's already here." Moxie could see the veterinarian's van parked by Willie's truck, waiting to take Pickle home.

69

The moment they came to a stop, Moxie jumped out and dashed in, heading straight for Misty's stall. She looked over the door. No Misty. In a panic, she swung open the gate, stepped inside, and looked in every corner.

"Oh, no," Moxie gulped. Were things worse than her parents had told her in Laramie? Had something really, really horrible happened to Misty?

She ran among the other stalls calling out, "Misty!" and searched each one. She stopped at Mozart's, where she found Dr. Johnson wrapping one of the horse's legs with a bandage.

"Oh, Dr. Johnson," she said, out of breath.

"Well, hello there, Moxie Wyoming." Dr. Johnson's kind eyes creased at the corners. "Just getting Mozart here fixed up, and she's going to be like new." He stroked the horse's back. "Guyetta and Skipper should be all right, too."

"But Dr. Johnson," Moxie wailed. "Where's Misty? I can't find her. What's happened to her?"

"I took care of Misty first and she's in the paddock behind the barn."

Moxie took off for the back of the barn at a full run.

"Don't you want to know how she's..." Dr. Johnson's voice trailed off as Moxie burst through the back door into the paddock.

Misty stood contentedly, her head down in the dish of oats at her feet, munching away. Her swayback looked more scooped out than ever, and her front legs were bandaged from right above her hooves up to her knees.

"Misty!" Moxie hollered.

Misty looked up, neighed, batted her skimpy eyelashes, and leaned down for another mouthful of oats.

Moxie ran over, threw her arms around Misty's neck, buried her face in the mare's gray-flecked coat, and began to snivel. "Misty, Misty, Misty..." A big sob erupted from her throat. "Please don't ever scare me like that again."

Moxie looked Misty straight in the eyes. "I thought I might never see you again." Then she noticed the scrapes all over Misty's face and touched one carefully. The horse pulled away; the wounds were tender and hurt.

"I'm so sorry." Moxie hugged her little mare. "Even with your face scratched up, you're still beautiful to me!"

Mike and Jane Woodson, both smiling, watched their daughter from the barn door as Dr. Johnson walked over to Misty and Moxie. "Now, young lady, your horse is going to be just fine."

The doctor put some ointment on his fingers and carefully applied it to Misty's face. "Here, you try it." Moxie dipped her fingers into the ointment and softly touched the mare's wounds.

"The horses got tangled in the barbed wire fence that was down. Some of them got their legs and faces all cut up, and they all bled a lot." Dr. Johnson leaned down to check Misty's bandages. "It looked much worse than it actually was."

He stood up. "I've already taken care of Guyetta and Mozart, but I still need to attend to Skipper's legs."

He reached out his hand. "Come with me, Moxie Wyoming. I'll teach you how to wrap their wounds, and you can practice on Skipper while I'm still here. That way you'll know how to take care of Misty's legs and make sure her bandages are always clean."

"I can do that!" Moxie gave Misty a kiss above her nose and walked into the barn with Dr. Johnson.

Chapter Thirteen

A week later, Misty's scratches were almost gone. Since the accident, Moxie Wyoming had dedicated herself to taking care of Misty's every need, from making sure the glitter bucket was always filled with fresh water to having plenty of treats on hand.

Each morning, Moxie had gently patted the ointment Dr. Johnson had given her onto the mare's wounds. She'd then carefully wrapped clean bandages around Misty's legs. They'd also regularly walked together in the pasture so the little horse wouldn't get too stiff while she healed.

Now Moxie found she had the rest of the day to herself. Pickle and Mrs. Turner had driven to Laramie for a visit to the dentist, and her own mom was running errands.

"Let's go for a little ride. How about it, girl? Feel ready with those legs?"

Misty neighed *yes* and stomped the ground twice.

So Moxie made a picnic and packed it in saddle bags. As she tied the leather bags to the back of Misty's saddle, she checked to make sure they hung evenly on each side of the saddle. The two walked out of the corral.

After a few minutes of leading Misty by the reins, Moxie flipped them over the horse's head and climbed on board. The two continued toward a grove of trees.

As they entered the shade of the pines and came to a stream, Moxie noted that Misty seemed a bit tired. "Ready for that picnic, girl?" Misty threw her head up and down, tapped the ground twice, and neighed. "Okay, there's a good spot over there."

Moxie directed Misty toward a log surrounded by good grass for munching. "Perfect," she said, dismounting.

After spreading a blanket for herself next to the log, Moxie pulled plastic containers from the saddle bags. She sat down in the middle of the blanket and organized the containers around her. On Misty's side, one container held carrots, one held sliced apples, and another had horse treats. On her side, she had a peanut butter and banana sandwich, chocolate chip cookies, and lemonade.

Moxie hopped up to give the little horse a carrot and then sat down to eat two bites of sandwich. She jumped up to feed Misty an apple slice and then plopped down to bite into a huge chocolate chip cookie. She sprang up again with horse treats and then dropped down on the blanket for another bite. Finally, she led Misty over to the stream for a drink while she gulped her lemonade.

"That was good, huh, girl?" Moxie said, as she walked Misty back to the picnic blanket. "So how about a nap?" Loud snores answered.

Moxie rolled her eyes, plopped onto the blanket, and pulled out a letter that had arrived that morning from her grandfather. She tore open the envelope and started reading.

Dear Moxie Wyoming,

Heard from your parents that you and Misty are getting along famously. That's fantastic! And now that you have the pink boots, I'm guessing that you've discovered something special happens when you wear them and ride Misty.

As you know, my mother, your great-grandmother, Rose Woodson, was a champion rodeo queen in the 1940s. She had those boots made to order by a famous bootmaker in El Paso. She wanted them to go with her all-pink rodeo outfits. I've enclosed a 1950 postcard showing her wearing the boots while riding in a barrel racing event. Not only was

my mom beautiful, she was a rider with impressive talents who won many first-place ribbons.

Then she discovered magical things happened when she wore the pink boots and rode her favorite horse. I never actually saw the magic...just heard the stories over the years.

By the way, I searched high and low for that mysterious bootmaker. I wanted to learn more about the magic, but I never could find him. What I do know from Granny Rose's stories is that she used this gift to help others, and she told me that gave her far more happiness than winning all those ribbons.

In the 1970s, my mother gave me the boots and asked me to save them for someone special, someone who could use the gift wisely. I've been waiting a long time to find that someone special, and Moxie Wyoming, I believe it's you.

Remember, if you intend to keep those pink boots, you must help others. And if you do, you'll make your great-grandmother, the Pink Rose of Texas, proud.

Love,
Grandpops

P.S. Nobody else knows about the magic!

Moxie looked at the old postcard and thought about how her rodeo champion great-grandmother used the magic pink boots to help others. This was a whole new side of Granny Rose to think about.

Chapter Fourteen

Some days later, Moxie Wyoming took Misty riding in the Snowies. After their first liftoff, Moxie quickly realized that she and her horse were a little rusty at flying together. As soon as they hit a couple of bumpy air currents, they found themselves bouncing up and down.

"Uuuugh, Misty," Moxie groaned and leaned on the horse's neck. "This is worse than a rollercoaster. I think I'm going to be sick..."

Misty landed as fast as possible and without a jolt. She stood patiently while her rider's normal color returned.

"I think we just need some practice." Moxie gave the mare a gentle kick. "Let's go!" They took off, and this time, the flying went much better—no more bumps, rollercoaster rides, or feeling sick.

The horse and rider landed, and Misty moved into a smooth lope. She took Moxie up a new canyon and through the woods along a trail the two of them had never ridden before.

After ten minutes, Misty slowed down to a walk. Moxie stretched her legs and wiggled her toes in the pink boots. The horse stopped suddenly, almost sending Moxie over her head.

"What's the matter, girl?" Moxie pushed herself off Misty's neck and back into the saddle. "Want a break?"

Misty pounded the ground once with her left leg.

"No, okay. So why did you stop?" And then Moxie grinned. "The Mustangs are close by, aren't they?"

The mare pounded the ground twice with her right leg.

"Are they up ahead?"

Misty stomped twice.

"Let's check it out." Moxie flattened herself against one side of the mare's neck so that Misty would look more like a horse with no rider.

The girl and horse rounded the bend. They walked quietly to a canopy of trees at the edge of a grassy flat.

Moxie and Misty paused silently at the edge of the meadow, watching a herd of twenty Mustangs peacefully eating the grass. A few of the horses stood quietly napping and nodded every now and then in their sleep.

Peeking over Misty's neck, Moxie gazed in wonder at several of the foals nestled closely against their mothers' sides. The smile on her face grew when she saw one little filly prance around on skinny young legs.

The beautiful palomino-colored stallion, who had been feeding on the far side of the grassy flat, stuck his head up and neighed loudly in Misty's direction.

Misty responded, also loudly.

Other members of the herd, including the chestnut lead mare with the black mane and tail, looked in Misty's direction.

The stallion trotted over, snorting and neighing more.

"Uh oh," Moxie stammered. "He's not going to be happy when he sees me."

But Misty and the stallion continued back and forth in a kind of horse conversation.

Misty neighed again and pushed her head toward Moxie, who got the message. "Okay, okay." She slowly sat up in the saddle.

The other horses took notice, too, and the herd began to make nickering sounds. Moxie felt twenty sets of eyes on her.

Even though Moxie held Misty's reins in her hands, she let the little mare lead the way through the herd. Moxie felt butterflies in her stomach when she saw some of the horses put back their ears. She knew it meant the Mustangs were alarmed, and she should be careful.

"Oh, Misty, they aren't happy about us being here. Do you think it's okay to just walk around?" Then to Moxie's surprise, their ears stood back up. "Uh, maybe they like us?"

Misty pounded twice, agreeing, and continued walking.

As she and Moxie rode through the herd, Misty whinnied quietly, greeting all the different horses. Moxie also greeted the animals in a low, gentle voice.

"Hi there, cutie-pie!" she said to one of the foals peeking out from behind her mother's legs.

"You are so beautiful!" she told a sturdy copper-red Mustang with a white streak, called a blazc, between his eyes and a wheat-colored mane and tail.

A smoky-colored filly pranced out in front of Misty, and Moxie giggled.

Misty sidled back up to the large, pale yellow stallion and glued herself to his side. The wild horse didn't seem nervous at all that Moxie was so close, so she took her feet out of the stirrups and sat sideways in Misty's saddle, leaning against the big stallion's back as if it were the back of a comfy sofa.

"I'm sure you're the boss," she said to him.

The lead mare threw her head from side to side and neighed in objection. "Except for maybe her," Moxie said.

She pointed to the chestnut-colored horse, looked her in the eye, and continued. "I'll call you Mamma Mia. Okay?"

The mare pounded the ground with her front hooves.

"I hope that's a *yes*," Moxie said, and then looked over at the stallion. "Anyway, I think I'll call you Rocky. It sounds strong, like you're in charge with Mamma Mia." She draped her arm along his back and rubbed his neck. "You like that name?"

The stallion looked at Moxie with his dark eyes and nickered, then looked at Misty, who batted her big eyes, which were once again thick with lashes.

The four of them walked together around the flat.

The rest of the herd fell in behind, with Misty, Moxie, Rocky, and Mamma Mia guiding the Mustangs. Misty was once again leading a herd, and Moxie Wyoming felt happy to be her friend.

Over the next few days, Moxie and Misty developed a routine. The Mustangs had a favorite mountain pond in the Snowies, so that became their regular picnic spot, too.

Each day, Moxie would pack a peanut butter and banana sandwich and lemonade in one saddle bag. The other she'd fill with apples and carrots for the herd.

During visits to the mountain pond, Misty stayed close to Rocky and the two ate grass together in the shade. And just as Rocky had accepted Misty's rider, Mamma Mia and the other wild horses also welcomed the girl.

Moxie would walk through the herd and offer apple slices and carrots to the Mustangs. At first the wild horses wouldn't take the food, but they changed their minds after watching Misty snacking.

Once she'd handed out the treats, Moxie would play and cuddle with the little foals.

These were blissful summer days for Moxie Wyoming, and she wanted them to last forever.

~~~~~

Back at the barn one evening, Misty slurped from the glitter-covered water bucket in her stall. Moxie and Pickle sat squished in the big armchair in Moxie's hangout, flipping through another big book about Mustangs.

"Misty?" Moxie called. The mare looked out from her stall toward Moxie and Pickle. "Did you know that some *wild Mustangs descended from*—I think that means, 'comes from'—*the horses brought* to *America by the Spanish*, uh..." She sounded out the next word. "*...con-quis-ta-dors*, or explorers?"

Pickle's eyes moved back and forth between Moxie and Misty as his best friend continued reading to the horse.

"And it says here that the word *Mustang* comes from the Spanish word *mesteño*. That means *horse without an owner*, or a stray. I guess like a stray dog."

"Um, are you reading to that horse?" Pickle asked. "Isn't that kinda weird?"

Embarrassed, Moxie quickly flipped through some pages. "I just talk to her the way I talk to Bunker or any of our animals. Don't you talk to *your* animals?"

"Yeah. But I say things like 'good girl' or 'supper-dupper time.' I don't read to them from books," he said. "I mean, it's not like Misty can understand you."

Moxie quickly glanced at Misty, who winked.

Moxie turned her attention to Pickle and shrugged. "And it also says here that in 1971 the U.S. Congress called the Mustangs *living symbols of the historic and pioneer spirit of the West*. Did you know that, Pickle Turner?"

Before her best friend could answer, Moxie slammed shut the book. "That's enough reading! Let's make popcorn."

Chapter Fifteen

Friday morning, Pickle, Bunker, and Pie, the barn cat, watched Moxie do her chores inside the chicken coop. The pecking chickens made Pickle nervous, and Bunker and Pie hated Rudy the rooster, so the three stood together outside the coop's fence as Moxie filled up the feeder.

"Pickle, this bag of feed is soooo heavy," Moxie fake-complained. "Come help me. Don't be such a *chicken!*"

Moxie Wyoming laughed at her own joke, and Pickle fake-laughed, too, rolling his eyes. The barn cat scooted away, only to pop up on top of the chicken coop's low roof.

Meanwhile, the rooster approached Bunker. The hair on the dog's neck and back stood up, and his low growl through the fence warned Rudy, *Don't come any closer.*

Watching the two, Pickle stepped back from the coop.

Rudy charged toward Bunker, who jumped up, barking and snarling. The rooster skidded to a stop right at the fence, flapping its wings and crowing. The cat screeched, jumped off the roof, and ran into the barn. Bunker, usually the world's most cuddly, lovable dog, continued his loud barking and growling.

"Rudy, cut it out!" Moxie yelled at the rooster. "Bunker, cool it! Settle down," she commanded her dog. While Rudy shifted his attention to some of the hens, Bunker stopped barking, looked at Moxie, and sat.

Pickle calmly folded his arms across his chest and said, "This is why I stay out here, while you're in there feeding those birds!"

Moxie gave Pickle her usual funny stare.

The sound of a car coming to the ranch diverted their attention. The kids watched a highway patrol cruiser pull up to the house.

"Moxie," Pickle said in a low voice. "That's the officer we saw at the rodeo and then at Jubilee Days."

"Quick, act busy," Moxie said. "I still can't figure him out. Is he helping those Jenkins guys, or up to something with the Curly T ranch?"

Pickle stepped into the coop and helped Moxie put away the bag of feed. "What if they're all working together?"

"I've been thinking about that, too, since none of them likes Mustangs. Except we don't really know about the officer. Anyway, I wonder what he wants," Moxie whispered.

They grabbed baskets and gathered eggs. "Do you think those men told him we know about that corral?" Pickle asked, reaching under a hen for an egg. "Ouch! Did you see that? That hen got me!"

"You've got to hold your basket in front of them while you reach in for the egg, so that they peck the basket instead of your hand, silly! Like this." Moxie demonstrated.

"Hey, kids! How's it going today?" the officer called out, walking in their direction. "I'd like to speak with you for a moment." Anxious, the kids exited the chicken coop and shuffled toward him.

"I'm Officer Brown of the Wyoming Highway Patrol." He reached out to shake their hands. Moxie took a deep breath, looked him in the eye, and firmly shook his hand, while Pickle tucked his hand in a pocket.

"Are your parents around?" he asked.

Thinking fast, she answered, "I'm Moxie Wyoming Woodson, and this is my best friend, Pickle Turner. My parents will be back any minute."

"Well, it's good to meet you." He gave Moxie and Pickle a slight nod. "I'm kind of new around here, just transferred to this area a few months ago." Moxie noticed his gaze sweep around the place, from the house to the barn to the chicken coop. It gave her the creeps.

The officer looked back at the kids. "I'm letting everybody know there will be some roadwork around here on Sunday morning and folks should avoid driving until noon, if possible."

"You mean don't drive out there?" Moxie pointed in the general direction of the highway.

"That's right, but the work's actually happening near the Deer Crossing turnoff," Officer Brown said and got into his car. Moxie and Pickle looked at each other, remembering the secret corral down that road.

Moxie grabbed Pickle's arm and ran up to the driver's side, but left plenty of space between them and the car window. "Uh, Officer, you said on Sunday, not Saturday, right? I want to be sure I remember the right day."

"Yes, young lady. The roadwork is on Sunday." He smiled at them. "Well, I've got to get going," he added.

"Yes, sir," the kids said in unison.

The officer reached out of the car window to hand each of them a small magnet. "Also, here's a new helpline for the public that we've added to our phones. Put it on your fridge. If you ever have any trouble, or you want to report anything strange...say you're home by yourselves and need help, the highway patrol will come out as fast as possible." He looked at the kids, smiled, and started the car engine. "It's our new Good Neighbor program."

"Thank you," Moxie said, while Pickle smiled tight-lipped at the ground. "We'll tell our parents."

Officer Brown drove away, and the kids walked back to the chicken coop. "No way would I call that guy for help," Moxie said under her breath.

"No way," Pickle agreed.

"Do you think they're really doing road work on Sunday, or is that the day of their roundup?" Moxie Wyoming said. "I wonder if Officer Brown is telling the truth or if it's all a big fat lie."

Chapter Sixteen

It was Saturday, and Moxie, her dad, and Pickle sat in the bleachers at the rodeo in Laramie. Pickle's cousin, Sue, had just won the barrel racing event again.

Moxie was daydreaming about being a barrel racing champion like Sue when her father suddenly waved at a couple coming up the steps in their section of the bleachers. It was Sam and Jamie Bingham. Moxie and Pickle nudged each other.

"Mike, how are you doing?" Mr. Bingham's face cracked a small smile. He looked over at Moxie and Pickle and eyed them a little suspiciously.

Moxie set her jaw firmly and looked back, while Pickle wilted a bit under the man's hard gaze. *The same way Jamie did,* Moxie thought. *He must be a really strict dad.*

Moxie's father stood up to shake hands with the leathery-skinned cowboy. "Hi Sam, Jamie." Mr. Bingham's daughter stood quietly behind her father, looking down.

Moxie's dad continued. "I don't believe you've met my daughter, Moxie Wyoming, and her best friend, Pickle Turner." He signaled for Moxie and Pickle to stand up. "Kids, this is Mr. Bingham and his daughter, Jamie, from the Curly T Cattle Ranch." They shook hands with the Binghams.

"Nice to meet you youngsters," Mr. Bingham said, and Moxie thought his voice sounded particularly rough and unfriendly. "Did you and the kids catch much of the barrel racing?" he asked.

"All of it," Moxie's dad answered. "We saw some mighty fine riding and some beautiful horses."

"My favorite horses are Mustangs," Moxie piped up, staring hard at both Binghams.

"I've got no use for them," Mr. Bingham muttered. "They're a nuisance to our cattle." He gestured toward Jamie and chuckled. "Although, my daughter here just isn't tough enough about those wild nags."

Jamie glanced around, looking nervous.

"Don't let her fool you," her father said. "She's always saying what she thinks I want to hear, that she doesn't like them—you know, trying to please the old man."

Jamie's already poor posture got even more slouchy.

Mr. Bingham went on, "But she's got a soft spot for those pests—"

Surprised by this news about Jamie, Moxie interrupted. "Mustangs are beautiful. How can you hate them?"

"That's enough, squirt," her father said softly. "Well, good to see you, Sam and Jamie. Enjoy the calf roping."

Sam Bingham nodded, and he and his daughter continued climbing the bleacher steps. Moxie watched them sit down and wondered what to make of Jamie. Did she really like Mustangs, or was she a phony?

They waited for calf-roping to start, and Moxie's eyes swept over the crowd milling around the corrals. Competitors checked out the bulls they would be riding after the calf roping, and fans gathered around, too.

Moxie's gaze stopped when she came to two familiar cowboys—Jeb and Frank Jenkins. She gasped, and her dad and Pickle turned to her in curiosity.

"Why are your eyes so big?" Pickle asked.

"You all right?" her father asked. "Did you swallow something? Need to cough?"

"I'm okay, Dad, just got a tickle in my throat." Moxie forced a fake cough. The two cowboys were talking to a bull rider. The rider

89

wore a protective vest and was sitting on a fence. "I need to get some water," she stammered. She coughed again, dramatically.

"Want me to come with you?" Pickle jumped up.

"Sure," Moxie said. "Be right back, Dad." She and Pickle quickly scooted away.

Dashing behind her, Pickle asked, "What's up?"

"The bad guys are here." Moxie Wyoming tugged on Pickle's sleeve. "Come on, let's see if they talk about their roundup."

Down below, the two friends snaked behind the bleachers and over to the corrals on the side of the rodeo ring. They stayed low so that Moxie's dad wouldn't spot them.

The kids slipped down a path between corrals filled with bulls and horses and tried not to attract attention. Soon, they spotted the Jenkins brothers' dusty-brown and gray-colored cowboy hats above the fences.

Moxie and Pickle could hear them talking to the bull rider, but couldn't understand what they were saying. The kids tiptoed closer and hid behind barrels next to the fence.

"...so, Jake, we thought we'd round up these Mustangs early tomorrow," Jeb said. "Most people are at church or sleepin' on a Sunday morning." Moxie and Pickle looked at each other and stayed quiet.

"Keep it down." Frank looked around, checking to make sure no one else could hear their plan.

Whoa! What if Jeb and Frank catch us listening, Moxie wondered.

Behind the barrels, the kids looked at each other with fear in their eyes. They continued listening to the brothers describe the secret corral to hold the eighty Mustangs they'd found scattered around the Snowies. They told Jake they had already picked up thirty-five horses and had their eye on another herd of twenty led by a big palomino stallion.

I knew it, Moxie thought, getting angry. *They want to capture Rocky's herd! These guys are bad news.*

"That's still a lot of horses for the three of us to round up," Jake said.

"We've got a couple of others helpin' in the morning," Frank answered.

Moxie wondered if Sam and Jamie Bingham were part of the Jenkins gang. Maybe Sam and Jamie were even the ones who'd tipped them off about Rocky's herd in the first place. Big phonies, yep, that's what they were.

"Whatcha gonna do with the horses once they're in the corral?" Jake asked.

"We've got a guy over in Cheyenne we're selling them to," Jeb said. "He'll trailer them out, and who knows what he'll do with them—"

"Probably no good, but that's his business, if you know what I mean." Frank laughed in an ugly way.

Moxie snuck a look. She thought Frank was squinting straight at her and so she ducked, pulling Pickle with her until they were flat on the ground. She peeked out carefully, but he hadn't seen her.

"What about people being nosy about a bunch of trailers?" Jake asked.

"We've got a special friend in the highway patrol keeping traffic out of the way Sunday morning." Frank smirked. "So, don't worry about that."

"Hey, is that smart, having him as the lookout?" Jake asked. "He's a law enforcement officer, you know. I mean, he could turn on you and arrest all of us."

"Don't worry about Officer Brown." Jeb leaned in as if he was telling them something secret. "Someone I know over by Rock Springs told me this cop is an okay guy." He put one boot up on the first rung of the fence. "So, are you in, Jake? We'll split the money from the sale of the horses."

"I'm in." Jake jumped down from the fence and shook their hands. "I can always count on you two to come up with a way to make some easy money."

"Remember, we don't want the sheriff to find out," Frank advised. "So keep it quiet."

Moxie and Pickle gulped and decided they'd better get out of there as quickly as possible. They stayed low and snuck back the same way they had come.

"They said their gang has six people," Moxie said as they walked through the crowd.

"Jeb and Frank," Pickle said. "And Jake and Clem. That's four."

"Want to bet who the other two gang members are?" Moxie asked. "How about Jamie and Mr. Bingham?"

"Yeah, they're probably in on it, too," Pickle answered, close on Moxie's heels.

"Well, the Binghams are at the rodeo, too. We just saw them," Moxie said. "They could have met up here with Jeb and Frank to go over their plan before the rodeo started."

At the bottom of the bleachers, Moxie stopped. "I just remembered something...uh, go tell Dad I'm using the restroom, so he doesn't come looking for me."

"Okay, but whatcha gonna do, Moxie?" Pickle asked, sounding worried.

"I need to find someone. I mean, call someone for help," Moxie said. "If only I had my own cell phone. Don't tell Dad anything about those guys. Okay?" Moxie's best friend nodded and went up the bleacher steps, glancing back with concern.

Moxie had to think fast. She thought about telling her father, but what if he went after those two creeps—Jeb with the nasty scar on his face and Frank with the crooked nose? She had no doubt those men were mean, and even without the rest of the gang, it would still be two against one. She didn't like that at all.

She finally found a pay phone and dug some money out of her pocket. For a second she thought about calling the new Good Neighbor helpline since she had memorized the number. But Officer Brown might get the call, and she didn't trust him.

Pulling out the card she'd gotten from *Miss Laramie Jubilee Days*, she quickly dropped some coins into the phone's slot and dialed the cell number.

"Uh, hi, Miss Hendricks?" Moxie whispered as soon as she heard the phone pick up, but it was voice mail. She waited for the beep to begin speaking. "Miss Hendricks, this is Moxie Wyoming Woodson. I met you with my friend Pickle at Laramie Jubilee Days." Moxie tried to stay calm, but urgency filled her voice. "Anyway, I've got a hot tip, since you want to be a deputy and all, and you like Mustangs."

The whole story came out in a rush, everything she had just heard Jeb and Frank say to Jake. "They're breaking the law, aren't they, Ms. Hendricks? Can't you arrest them?"

Explaining directions to the corral, the girl talked fast, worried the voice mail would beep and stop recording. She then covered her mouth and the mouthpiece of the phone. "They didn't see me at the rodeo and don't know I'm calling you. I was real careful."

Moxie looked around to make sure no one could overhear. "I heard them say some guy from Cheyenne is going to pick up the Mustangs tomorrow. The Jenkins guys said they'd split the money with the rest of the gang, even with that highway patrol guy, Clem Brown. He's the lookout for them."

Moxie got a tickle in her throat, a real one this time, and coughed. "Excuse me. I'm so not making this up, Miss Hendricks, promise. Please keep it a secret that it's me calling you. I don't want to get into trouble for being nosy. Okay, that's it. Maybe you can help. Bye." And she hung up the phone.

Moxie looked around and noticed Jeb and Frank Jenkins walking in her direction. She scurried up into the bleachers to sit as close as possible to her dad.

"What took so long?" Her dad squeezed her shoulder. "I almost sent the sheriff out looking for you."

Moxie felt herself freeze up, stiff as a board.

"It was just a joke, kiddo," her dad reassured her and looked at her quizzically. "Are you okay?"

"Yeah, Dad," Moxie croaked and glanced at Pickle with a quick shake of her head.

Moxie tried to focus on the rest of the calf roping and bull riding, but she could hardly wait to get home that evening. She needed to come up with a plan between tonight and tomorrow morning. She had to figure out how she and Misty could help Rocky and his herd stay away from the roundup.

She snuck a look up the bleachers at Sam and Jamie Bingham. Sam talked quietly to his daughter, who looked down and nodded. *I bet they're talking about the Sunday roundup with the Jenkins brothers,* she thought.

~~~~~

Moxie never got a chance to tell Pickle about her phone message to Mary Lou Hendricks. She'd wanted to brainstorm ideas to save the herd with her best friend, but no such luck. Instead, she sat on her bed by herself, trying to come up with a plan. Nothing. What should she do? Well, a snack always helped.

On her way to the kitchen, she looked at the portrait at the bottom of the front hall steps, and sighed. *What should I do, Granny Rose? I'm just one kid. How can I save all of those horses?*

All of a sudden, her grandmother's beautiful black horse in the painting winked at her!

Moxie froze and stared at the horse. *Wait a minute, What just happened?* she thought. *How can a painting wink? I only know one horse who winks, and that's Misty!*

She pulled a chair over and stood on it to get a closer look. For the first time, Moxie noticed that Granny Rose's horse looked a lot like Misty when she was flying—very black and without any gray, a thick mane and tail, and bright, alert eyes framed by thick lashes.

The girl reached out to touch the shadow of a white sock on the horse's back left leg and was surprised that the canvas felt warm. She pulled her hand back quickly, then reached out to pat the young horse's bushy mane.

"Misty, is that really you? Were you...were you Granny Rose's horse, too?"

The moment Moxie's finger felt the canvas again, the horse winked once more, and the girl gasped.

"It is you!" Moxie Wyoming beamed her biggest grin.

She quickly left the house, walking to the barn in her PJs and pink cowboy boots. She carried a pillowcase stuffed with her pink riding tights and slicker. Moxie felt sneaky and didn't like keeping secrets from her parents, but after what had just happened in front of the painting, she was now positive that she had to help the Mustangs. She was also certain that Misty would keep her safe.

When she got to the barn, Moxie exclaimed, "That's you in the painting with Granny Rose, isn't it, girl?"

Misty pounded *yes* with her hoof in reply.

"I knew it!" She kissed Misty on the nose. "You're even older than I thought when you first came." She laughed. "More Misty magic!"

Then Moxie got back to work figuring out a plan, pacing between their two stalls, back and forth, back and forth.

"Do you know a special hiding place where we can take Rocky and the herd?"

Misty's head moved back and forth, watching her.

"I guess we'll figure out a hiding place once we find Rocky and his herd. Okay?"

Misty pounded the ground twice and snorted quietly, and Moxie thought her little horse looked calm and peaceful.

"Do you know something I don't know?" she asked her.

But Misty just batted her skimpy eyelashes.

"Whatever." Moxie unrolled her sleeping bag. "First, we need to get out of here really early, ride up to the Snowies, and warn Rocky and the herd that those cowboys are coming." She set her alarm clock. "How about 4 a.m.?"

Misty made a low nickering sound and stared hard at Moxie. "Okay, okay." Moxie reset her alarm clock. "4:45. No later." She plopped down on the sleeping bag and punched her pillow to get it just right. "Now get some sleep."

But Misty was already snoring.

"Geez, wake up the whole barn, while you're at it." Moxie took the pillow and put it over her head, trying to drown out her horse's snores.

Chapter Seventeen

Very early the next morning, Moxie quietly led Misty out to the corral, saddled and ready to go. Once they were in the field behind the barn, Moxie climbed onto her horse. They walked in the direction of the Snowies as the pre-dawn light began to illuminate the black sky.

"Oh, Misty. We gotta help Rocky and the herd." She grabbed Misty's mane with one hand, and gave her a gentle kick with her pink boots. "Okay, let's go."

Misty and Moxie Wyoming took flight and soon sailed over the foothills of the Snowies. Before long, they spotted a group of riders. "Look, there's the Jenkins gang! They got up before we did. Ugh! Maybe even three o'clock in the morning."

In the darkness below, Moxie could just make out five cowboys on horseback heading up a trail to higher ground.

"Misty, the sky is getting brighter. I think we need to be invisible so they don't see us up here." Before Moxie could even finish the sentence, she felt a quiver as the little mare snorted once and twitched her ears.

"We've just got to find the herd before they do," Moxie said as they flew over the riders.

Once the girl and her horse had passed the gang, Misty snorted and twitched her ears back and forth. "Does that mean we aren't invisible anymore?"

Misty snorted twice for *yes*, and Moxie giggled.

They flew beyond the foothills, higher into the mountains. Not far up a canyon, Moxie and Misty spotted the wild horses getting a drink from a mountain lake. As the early morning sun peeked over the horizon, Misty threw out her four legs in order to twirl and helicopter down for a soft landing in the middle of the herd.

Rocky and Mamma Mia loped over to them. Before Moxie could say a word, Misty pounded the ground with both legs and snorted, looking straight at Rocky. The stallion looked back into Misty's eyes and responded with nervous snorts of his own.

"Come on, Rocky!" she hollered. "Come on, Mama Mia! Follow us!" She and Misty rode across the meadow toward a different trail from the one the cowboys were using. Mama Mia neighed and followed, and the other horses fell in behind. Rocky neighed even louder, rearing and pounding the ground with his front hooves. Then he took off and brought up the back of the herd.

The Jenkins gang rode into Moxie's view, and they quickly spotted her on Misty, leading the horses. Strangely—maybe it was more of Misty's magic—but Moxie Wyoming could hear every word the two men said, even though they were far off. "Hey, Frank!" Jeb took off his hat and slapped his leg with it as they rode on. "I don't believe it. Is that who I think it is?"

"Yep. I'm pretty sure it's that same kid, still on her scrawny, old horse. What's she doin' up here?" Frank hollered, riding alongside his brother. "Whatever. This time, no more Mr. Nice Guy."

"Right! She and that poor excuse for a horse are a real pain," Jeb yelled back. The riders galloped toward the same trail that Misty, Moxie, and the Mustangs planned to use.

The cowboys were rapidly gaining on them. Moxie was scared they might cut off the escape path. She pulled out the gold whistle and blew it as hard as she could.

Misty and the other galloping horses didn't seem to notice the sound of the whistle blowing, so Moxie blew it again, and then a third time. She wasn't sure it would help, but she figured it was worth a try to find out if the grizzly bear was nearby.

Moxie and Misty let Mama Mia, the herd, and Rocky race onto the path first, and they followed. The Jenkins gang had missed cutting them off, but they were still in hard pursuit, closing up the distance between the two groups.

"Hey, girl, where do you think you're headin' with those Mustangs?" Frank yelled. "Those are our horses! We'll teach you a lesson—"

Suddenly, the huge grizzly bear with the notched ear lumbered out from behind a thicket of trees and stepped right onto the path. The monstrous bear put himself between Moxie and the Jenkins gang.

Jeb and Frank, along with the others, skidded to a stop, gawking at the ferocious bear. Moxie looked over her shoulder just in time to see the animal stand up and roar fiercely.

The riders immediately turned their horses around and took off, the grizzly now running right after them. Moxie Wyoming fist-pumped the air.

As she and Misty continued leading the Mustangs, Moxie realized something was different about this ride. This time, her horse rode like the wind down *on* the ground, not *above* it, guiding the herd away from danger.

As they galloped, Moxie also noticed that *all* the horses seemed to ride at the same super-fast speed as she and Misty. Had her little mare cast a magic spell on the entire herd? The forests, meadows, mountains, scrubby canyons, and stretches of desert-like terrain streaked by. Moxie felt as if they were all in a magical, high-speed tunnel of wind.

Moxie guessed they'd been riding several hours because it seemed they'd traveled quite a distance. But the sun was still low in the sky, just creeping above the horizon. *That's weird*, she thought.

Moxie Wyoming didn't have a clue where they were going, but she wasn't scared. Misty was in charge, and she trusted her mare and felt safe riding her in this odd tunnel.

Finally, Misty slowed to a gentle lope, and the herd did the same. The scenery stopped streaking by, and Moxie guessed they were out of the strange tunnel that had allowed them to ride so fast.

They slowed down even more, now walking on a beat-up dirt road. Moxie noticed the road didn't look as if it was used much anymore since it was overgrown with tall grasses.

She saw a gate up ahead with a sign, and as they got closer she read it aloud. "Darwin Ranch, Private Property." Moxie sat up straight in the saddle with surprise. "This is where you used to live, Misty, isn't it?"

Moxie pulled on the reins to tell Misty to stop. "Did we ride all the way from the Snowies to the Gros Ventre Mountains?"

Misty snorted, pounding the ground twice.

"But that's clear across the state, almost four hundred miles! How'd we get here so fast?" Moxie asked. "Must be that strange tube of air we were in."

Moxie started to dismount. "Misty, do you want me to open the gate so that we can visit? Are you trying to tell me you're homesick?"

But Misty took a hard right turn from the road and Moxie Wyoming almost tipped off the saddle as they moved into the aspen grove nearby. She continued to let Misty lead the way with the Mustang herd right behind them.

A wispy cloud settled over the group, like it was protecting them. Sunbeams cut through the cloud and made their ride feel even more mysterious and enchanted.

As the sun's rays hit the ground around them, the early morning dew sparkled on the underbrush like diamonds. Moxie felt certain she was riding someplace special. Up ahead, over the tops of the aspens, she could see a rock cliff.

When she and Misty and the Mustangs emerged from the trees, they faced the huge cliff. They looked up, and it seemed to touch the sky. Moxie saw no way to continue forward. The cliff also seemed to stretch for miles in both directions. "Now what do we do?"

Misty turned left and walked along the rocky wall. She halted at a spot covered by scrubby branches. The horse snorted and neighed, and the herd neighed back.

Misty pounded the ground three times with her right hoof and once with her left.

"What's going on?" Moxie wondered aloud. Then Misty neighed while circling once in place.

The scraggly branches curled back, revealing a crack in the cliff. At the same time, a glow in the crack began pulsing like a flashing warning light as the opening grew wider. Moxie nervously squirmed in her saddle, but she couldn't take her eyes off the shimmering light.

Then Misty carried Moxie Wyoming through the glowing crack into a stone tunnel, and the rest of the horses followed behind.

Chapter Eighteen

Moxie, Misty, and the Mustangs rode single file down the narrow passageway. "Where are you taking us?" Moxie whispered. She didn't like this cramped place at all.

Misty whinnied softly, as if to say, *It's okay.*

Then Moxie saw light up ahead. "Are we there?"

They rode toward an opening and burst into bright sunlight. The group stopped and took in the vast panorama. Directly in front of them stood a tall, wooden arch with a sign.

Dizzy Humphrey's Animal Shelter

Somebody had painted the letters with glitter on the top of the arch, and the name sparkled in the sun.

Moxie's eyes swept past the arch and across the most beautiful meadow she had ever seen. She saw fields of lush green grasses filled with flowers: red Indian paintbrush, pink wild roses, bluish-purple silvery lupine, yellow black-eyed Susans, and many more.

From a nearby grove of aspen trees, the heart-shaped leaves trembled in the breeze and made a lovely rustling sound. Birds flitted and sang among the branches.

The entire basin was surrounded by red rock cliffs, creating a craggy, rocky fence around the valley. Above the cliffs were more of the same fluffy clouds that Moxie had seen during the ride. Three brilliant rainbows swept across the sky. They began in the same sparkling pond but shot out in different directions.

Misty led the Mustangs to the pond for a drink, and all the horses reached down to slurp the cool water. Moxie stretched up in the saddle, making herself as tall as possible. *Who was this Dizzy Humphrey,* she wondered, *and where was the building for the animal shelter?*

"Where *are* we?" She scanned the landscape in every direction and began to notice many different creatures scattered across the valley.

"Hey, Misty, look at all those animals. I've never seen a giraffe in Wyoming! Or a lion!" She tugged on the reins to pull Misty's head up from the water to look. "*So* weird, they all seem to like each other. Like the lion hanging out next to the baby giraffe over there. Shouldn't they be fighting or something?"

A voice startled her from behind. "Here at the shelter, all the animals live in harmony."

She turned. A girl with red pigtails and freckles across her nose stood on a tree stump. "You shouldn't sneak up on people," Moxie instructed. She thought they were the same age. "Who are you?"

"I'm Dizzy Humphrey." The girl nodded toward the mare. "I know Misty. She's come here lots of times. Who are you?"

"I'm Moxie Wyoming." Moxie looked curiously at her horse. "She has? I mean, she's come here a lot?"

"Yeah, with other animals," Dizzy said.

"Oh!" Moxie thought about that for just a moment, then jumped down from the saddle and gestured to the herd. "Misty and I are trying to save these Mustangs and keep them safe from some mean cowboys."

"Well," Dizzy said, "you've come to the right place. No one will find them here."

"I saw the sign over there..." Moxie pointed in the direction of the tall wooden arch. "...Dizzy Humphrey's Animal Shelter. At home, my mom took me to an animal shelter where we got our dog, Bunker, and it's in a building in Laramie. Where's your building?"

"We have buildings for the animals when they need them, mostly sheds and barns. They're all over the valley, just not right here. You see, this whole valley..." Dizzy spun around on the stump, her arm sweeping the air around her. "...and everything inside this cliff wall are part of the refuge."

"So how come your name's on the sign?" Moxie asked. "I mean, you're just a kid like me."

"Well, I love animals, and I've been rescuing them for a long, long, long time," Dizzy answered with a twinkle in her eye. "So I decided to create a special place—"

"That's cool," Moxie interrupted. "But why is that lion being so nice to the little giraffe? And don't they both usually live in Africa, not here in the Rocky Mountains?"

"A man brought them from Africa to California for his own private amusement park. But he didn't have enough money to take care of them. We got the word, and rescued them."

"So, why isn't the lion attacking the giraffe?" Moxie paused, as something else caught her eye. "And over there!"

Moxie and Dizzy watched a rabbit hop on the back of a red fox. "What's up with that? I thought foxes chased rabbits. They do where I come from."

"Well, Moxie Wyoming," Dizzy said. "This is a very unusual place, there's nowhere else like it."

"Why?" Moxie stepped up on a stump next to Dizzy, and the two stood eye to eye. "What's the deal here?"

"It's special. Animals who are in danger in other places can live here peacefully and always be safe."

"But I still don't get it," Moxie said, bewildered.

"See those sunbeams shooting through the big clouds near the cliffs?" Dizzy asked, and Moxie nodded. "Those are Harmony Sunbeams."

An owl landed on Dizzy's outstretched arm, while a group of Monarch butterflies settled on her shoulder. "All the animals come through the Harmony Sunbeams as they travel to the refuge. You rode through them on your way here."

"What happens when the sunbeams touch you? Is it like when the doctor takes an X-ray to make sure you didn't break a bone?"

"No." Dizzy giggled. "The Harmony Sunbeams make all creatures, big and small, act friendly toward each other." She shook her shoulder, and the butterflies moved to the owl's head, covering it like a funny hat.

"So we've been blasted by Harmony Sunbeams! Neat!" Moxie grinned from ear to ear. "But why aren't more people trying to come here?"

"Because we're invisible to people *outside*."

"Cool!" Moxie cooed. She loved that those cowboys wouldn't ever be able to find her Mustangs. But Moxie did wonder why *she* could see it. Was it because she was with Misty?

Dizzy took Moxie's hand. "I know you have questions. Come on." They hopped down from their stumps. "I'll give you a tour!"

Chapter Nineteen

Moxie Wyoming left Misty with the herd and spent the next few hours following Dizzy around the shelter. Many different kinds of animals were living there, with plenty of space for all of them.

"Hey, Dizzy. If animals keep coming here, when do you run out of room?"

"Never."

"How come?"

"Just one more reason this place is special." Dizzy's eyes twinkled. "Come on. There's more to see!"

In one woodsy area, Moxie counted eight baby foxes, known as kits, chasing each other up and down a huge mound while the mamma fox sat on top of the earthen hump watching over them. The mound was the root ball of a gigantic fallen tree, and Moxie saw that it made a nice den for the fox family.

"A farmer in New Jersey wanted to get rid of those foxes because he was worried they'd kill his chickens," Dizzy said. "That's why they're here."

"They came all the way from New Jersey?" Moxie said, amazed. "That's so far away."

"Our animals come from everywhere!" Dizzy told Moxie with pride. "Come on."

The two hiked to a clearing with a hut near the edge of the trees. A spotted fawn was prancing around a white duck and a brown rabbit. When they saw Moxie and Dizzy, all three scrambled into the hut.

"Let's get closer," Dizzy said to Moxie. As they approached the hut, four heads peered out to stare at them. A beagle with big floppy ears had joined in.

"Who are they?" Moxie asked.

"The beagle is Pumpkin. She's from a pound in North Carolina. The little fawn is Janie. She was an orphan found in a field in Michigan."

Dizzy kept walking while she explained. "The rabbit is Benjamin. He was left behind in a closed-up pet store in Tennessee. And the white duck is Dora. She just showed up one day."

A fifth head, that of a black Labrador retriever, stood out protectively above the group. "And that's Fizz! She was found locked in a shed in Oregon, starving and afraid of people," Dizzy said. "But look at her now!"

The girls stood by the opening of the hut and watched Fizz stretch out on the ground. The others lay as close as possible to her. Moxie and Dizzy giggled while Fizz licked and cuddled and kissed Pumpkin, Janie, Benjamin, and Dora.

"Fizz greets all the animals who come here, and she makes it her business to especially take care of the babies and the ones who show up alone." Dizzy's voice was filled with great tenderness.

The two youngsters continued walking through the woods until they came to another clearing. Moxie found herself staring at a big wall that looked gray and leathery. She touched it, and suddenly a leg stomped and caused the ground to rumble. She jumped back, looking up at massive ears and a long trunk swaying back and forth.

"That's Herman." Dizzy laughed. "He came from a circus in Mexico, where he was getting too old to perform."

"Wow!" Moxie's eyes were huge as she looked up at the enormous elephant. "How'd you sneak *him* up here? He's ginormous!"

"Yep, he was a tough case, getting him here from south of the border," Dizzy said. "Actually, Misty helped us on this one."

"She did?" Moxie said in awe, wondering how.

~~~~~

The girls sat by a brook, enjoying a picnic of tasty cinnamon rolls and apple juice. Afterward, Moxie and Dizzy played hide-and-seek with some of the younger residents of the shelter. The group included a golden retriever puppy, a thoroughbred foal, a Siamese kitten, a brown bear cub, a coyote pup, a gosling—or baby goose—and three Rhode Island Red chicks.

The little ones formed a circle and closed their eyes while Dizzy and Moxie found hiding places. After the seekers had stood still as long as they could, the puppy barked three times, and the group scattered to search.

No matter where the girls chose to hide, it never took more than thirty seconds for some of the small creatures to sniff them out. Then the entire group would tumble and swarm over the girls, causing fits of laughter. Finally, the animals dropped to the ground, tired from their game.

The girls also stretched out on the ground and gazed up at the sky. Moxie Wyoming counted clouds. "Hey, Dizz, if other people can't see the shelter, how come I can?"

"You're wearing the pink boots."

"You mean if I didn't have them on, I couldn't see this place?" Moxie pushed herself up on her elbows.

"Right," Dizzy answered. "And maybe you've already found out—no pink boots, no flying on Misty."

"Yeah," Moxie agreed. "I tried one day in my brown boots, and it didn't work." Then she sat up all the way. "How come Misty can fly?"

Dizzy sat up, too. "I can't explain it, but Misty definitely has the power."

"Guess I'd better take really good care of Misty and these boots so I can come back and visit."

~~~~~

Moxie and Misty stood in the midst of the wild Mustangs, saying their goodbyes. Fizz, the black Lab, and her animal friends ran among the newly arrived herd, welcoming them. The friendly dog kissed and nuzzled the foals, who scampered around in a tizzy.

"Now, Moxie, you and Misty can visit any time you miss Rocky and the herd." Dizzy squeezed Moxie's shoulder.

"Thanks. I know we will, won't we, girl?" Moxie looked at her mare, who snorted in approval. "And we'll want to see the other animals, too. And you!"

"I have an idea." Dizzy said with a gleam in her eye. "How'd you like to help us? You know, when an emergency comes up with other animals that need rescuing?"

"Absolutely, positively!" Moxie exclaimed. "Misty and I for sure want to help!"

"I'm going to make you official by having you recite the oath for a small club we have. The other club members help us when we have animal emergencies." Dizzy's eyes crinkled. "Are you ready?"

Moxie got serious and stood up tall. "Yep, I'm ready."

Fizz the Labrador and the other animals all stood in a line next to Dizzy. Moxie and Misty stood opposite them. The Mustang herd created a circle around the group, and other animals made an even larger circle around them.

"Repeat after me," Dizzy said. "I, Moxie Wyoming, promise to help any animals that need to be rescued from danger, hunger, or abuse." Moxie said the words slowly and clearly.

"I may bring animals in need to the shelter," Dizzy continued, "but I will never, ever tell anyone about this place."

Again, Moxie recited the words slowly and clearly, and added, "I swear on puppies and peanut butter. Wa-hoo!"

"You are now an official member of our club!" Dizzy said.

Misty neighed, while Moxie and Dizzy bounced together in a circle, hugging each other and giggling.

Fizz barked, Pumpkin howled, Dora quacked, and all the horses joined in Misty's neighing.

"This is a big honor, Dizz," Moxie said. "Thank you. But how will I know when you need us to help you?"

"Believe me, you'll know," Dizzy said. "Plus you'll get a secret password."

Chapter Twenty

As Moxie Wyoming and Misty rode back through the secret tunnel and came out the opening in the cliff, the mare snorted with excitement, threw her head around, and flicked her tail every which way.

"Happy, girl?" Moxie asked, stroking her mare's neck. "Now Rocky and the Mustangs will be safe. And they'll have fun with all their new friends!"

Misty pranced, launching Moxie into a giggle-fest. "Are you ready to go home?"

The little horse twirled in circles and let out the loudest neigh Moxie had ever heard.

In the distance, she heard another horse neighing in response. "Who's that?"

And then a chorus of neighing rose over the entire area. Misty's ears twitched in every direction, and she kicked up her back legs. "Ooops, Misty! Was that a little happy bucking?"

Moxie clung to the saddle's horn while off in the distance, the neighing continued. "Are those your buddies from the Darwin Ranch?"

Moxie gave a slight nudge, and her horse dashed into the aspen trees. "Whoa, Misty. Slow down! We'll get there soon enough."

She grabbed her mare's mane as they loped along a well-worn dirt path. Clearly Misty had galloped down this trail many times before.

As rider and horse entered a meadow, horses galloped in from the other side, led by a light-brown version of Misty. *That has to be Bandit,* Moxie decided, *Misty's son.* His face looked the same, and he rode fast like Misty but didn't have his mother's extreme swayback.

When they all met up in the middle of the field with lots of snorting and snickered greetings, Moxie quickly understood her little mare had reunited with friends and family. Thinking of one of her letters from Grandpops, Moxie recognized many of the other horses, too.

Misty ran straight over to a very dark brown draught horse and nuzzled his neck. He was gigantic. "You must be Hector!" Moxie exclaimed. "I heard all about you, how you threw off a very big man who was a guest at the Darwin." She giggled. "And then everybody started calling you Hector the Ejector!"

The two horses, one so huge and one so small, stood next to each other. "But mostly I know that you're Misty's protector, and that she loves you very much."

On the outer edges of the herd was the cutest little butterscotch pony with a blond mane and tail. The pony was kicking up a storm. "Now you cut that out, Heber!" Moxie shook her finger at the small horse. "Stop being such a show off."

Heber stopped and looked at the girl sitting on top of Misty. "That's right, I've heard all about you, too, that you're very spoiled by all the guests," Moxie said. Heber trotted up to Moxie for a scratch behind the ears.

Misty and Hector walked among the rest of the horses, so that Moxie, still in the saddle, could meet the herd. The horses included: Bishop, Monica, Deanza, Felicia, Quarter, Murray, Chaps, Nickel, Peanut Butter, Alice, Sage, Dusty, Vanessa, and Spot—all of Misty's old buddies.

Then Bandit walked up to his mother. "Oooh, you are so cute!" Moxie cooed. "I can't believe I'm meeting your son, Misty!" She leaned over from her saddle to rub Bandit's neck.

The three horses—Bandit, Hector, and Misty—walked at the front of the herd and then loped as they started the familiar ride back to the Darwin Ranch. Misty and Moxie Wyoming galloped into the lead, and Moxie hollered, "Misty, you're *still* queen of the herd!"

~~~~~

After splitting off from Bandit, who led the Darwin horses back to their ranch, Misty and Moxie pushed off to fly home. Moxie had to rush to get back before anyone missed them. Misty seemed to understand this and flew faster. She and Moxie streaked through the sky, heading for the Moose Creek Ranch.

As they approached the foothills of the Snowies, Moxie's curiosity got the better of her. "Misty, let's check out the secret corral and see what's going on down there. I hope the sheriff got my message from Mary Lou, since Jeb and Frank probably rounded up a lot of other Mustangs. At least they didn't get Rocky and his herd."

The two sailed down the canyon and came to the corral, where Misty circled above. Moxie saw wild horses impatiently moving around within the crowded enclosure. Two huge trucks with horse trailers were parked near the corral.

"Look, Misty, the sheriff did get the message." From her bird's-eye-view up high, Moxie watched the sheriff and his deputies quietly come up the road, some on horseback and others in vehicles. Without waiting for Moxie to ask, Misty quivered and twitched her ears, and Moxie knew they were invisible to those on the ground, just in case anyone looked up at the sky.

As the sheriff got close to the corral, one of the Jenkins crew realized they were about to be arrested and yelled to the others. The five gang members quickly jumped on their horses and galloped up the canyon trail, making a fast getaway.

"Yikes, Misty! Look at them go!" Moxie held on tight as Misty flew up the canyon. "The sheriff might not catch those guys if they hide up in the mountains. How can we help so they don't escape?"

Moxie and Misty soon soared over and past the Jenkins gang. Misty quivered again, and Moxie knew they could now be seen.

"I've got an idea, and it's hanging around my neck," Moxie said, as she touched the gold chain. "Look, land over there. That's the perfect spot!"

She pulled out the gold whistle on the end of the chain, while Misty gently helicoptered down. The second they landed on a grassy spot next to the trail, Moxie blew on the whistle as hard as she could.

Way down the path, Moxie Wyoming saw the first gang member come around a bend. She blew a second time on the whistle.

The rest of the gang came into view. Even though the five were still a ways from her, Moxie could see that Jeb and Frank Jenkins were in the lead. She couldn't tell who the others were, but they were riding hard, so she blew the gold whistle a third time.

As they got closer, Jeb and Frank came to a fast stop, which caused a chain reaction as the others pulled up on their reins, too.

"What's the problem? Why don't we keep going?" Jake from the rodeo hollered from the back.

"Frank, it's that girl with the whistle again!" Jeb looked nervously around the area, peering into the trees.

"Who is that girl, and why does she always show up and get in our way?" Frank growled to himself. But just like last time, Moxie could hear every word.

"Why are you so nervous, Jeb?" Jake asked. "You're looking around like you're expecting someone." He glanced back down the path. "I don't know about you, but I'm not waiting for the sheriff to get here." He looked at the other two gang members. "You coming?" They nodded, and the three of them started moving. Misty and Moxie watched and listened.

"I wouldn't do that if I were you," Jeb warned them.

"Come on. It's only a little girl on a scrawny nag." Jake rode by the brothers. "We'll just blow right past her." The three continued toward Moxie and Misty.

"Big mistake," Frank warned, but he and Jeb followed.

Moxie Wyoming and Misty stood their ground. The young rider sat up very straight in the saddle, looking confidently at the gang as they got near. She could now see all five riders clearly, Jeb, Frank, and Jake, but *not* Jamie or Sam Bingham. Instead there were two cowboys she'd never seen before.

"Misty, the Binghams are *not* here," Moxie said, keeping her voice down. "I was wrong about them being part of this roundup, but they sure did seem suspicious."

Misty pounded the ground twice in agreement.

"I guess Mr. Bingham is just a grumpy rancher who hates Mustangs. And maybe Jamie really does like wild horses, you know, the way I do."

Without warning, when the five riders were fifty-feet from her, they came to a sudden stop, frightened looks on their faces. Moxie smiled sweetly at them.

Jeb looked at Frank and said, "I'd rather take my chances with the sheriff. What about you?"

"I'm with you." Frank turned his horse at the same time as Jeb, and the two kicked their horses into an immediate gallop. The other three did the same, and they all raced down the path. Moxie was amazed that she and Misty could scare them away so easily.

By the time the Jenkins gang reached the bend, Moxie saw the sheriff and some of his deputies arriving. All the members of the gang stopped and put up their hands to surrender.

Moxie turned Misty to ride into the trees so the deputies wouldn't spot her. And that was when she discovered the real reason the gang had taken off so fast. The grizzly bear with the notched ear sat on a huge boulder close by.

"It's about time, Grizz. That's what I'm calling you, by the way." Moxie grinned. "I thought maybe you were going to be a no-show." She rode by him, and Misty batted her eyes at the bear. Grizz got down from the boulder and ran alongside the horse and rider.

119

"No wonder those guys looked so scared and rode straight to the sheriff," Moxie went on. "I'm not exactly ferocious like you." The three of them moved into the trees with Moxie Wyoming chattering nonstop to her new friend.

After saying goodbye to Grizz, Misty and Moxie rode directly home. Once at the barn, Moxie dismounted.

As the two silently walked into the back of the building, she glanced at the clock on the wall. It was only 8 a.m.! They had left very early, a little after 4:45. How could she and Misty have traveled so far and done so much in only three hours? Was that even possible?

Misty whinnied softly, as if she knew her rider's thoughts.

Moxie pulled off the saddle and hung it on a peg outside the stall, the little mare's eyes following her. "Maybe you get it, Misty, but I don't."

She filled the glitter bucket with water and brought it to her horse. "The important thing is that we saved Rocky and the Mustangs. Wait 'til I tell Pickle how we helped the sheriff catch the bad guys!"

Chapter Twenty-One

Moxie Wyoming wandered into the kitchen for breakfast, yawning as if she'd been sleeping in and had just awakened. She found Pickle sitting at the table, while Moxie's mother poured orange juice into glasses. Her father, talking on the phone, mixed batter in a bowl. Then he handed the bowl to her mom, who ladled the batter into a pan to make the pancakes. With the phone propped between his shoulder and ear so he could listen, Moxie's father hunted for a pen.

"Morning, Moxie. Pancakes?" her mom asked. Rubbing her eyes and pretending to still be sleepy, Moxie nodded, sat at the table, and gave her best friend the stare.

"You sure look grouchy! Why are you giving me the evil eye?" Pickle asked. "My parents are busy with a sick cow, so your mom invited me—"

"Shhh," Moxie whispered, motioning to her dad who was still talking.

"...what time did the sheriff pick them up?" he asked into the phone. "Clem Brown, too? I guess you never know about some people." Stretching, Moxie cautiously peered through half-open eyelids at her dad.

"Uh-huh...yeah." Her father listened. "Near the Deer Crossing turnoff...Really? Hmmm." Her dad scribbled on a pad. "How'd they find out?"

Moxie sat very still at the table, sure the game was up. Pickle looked at her curiously.

"Tip-off from a confidential caller? Wow," he said. Moxie's eyes popped open, and Pickle's, too.

"Okay, Willie. I'm glad they got to them before they shipped those Mustangs out of the country. Keep us posted. Bye." Her dad hung up and joined the kids at the table.

"What happened, Mr. Woodson?" Pickle tried his best to sound casual, as if he hadn't overheard the Jenkins brothers at the rodeo the night before. "What Mustangs?"

Moxie's mother put a plate of hot pancakes and a pitcher of warm maple syrup in the middle of the table.

"Yeah, what Mustangs?" Moxie asked.

"Well, good morning, squirt," her father said, reaching for the pancakes. "How many pancakes would you kids like?"

"Two, please," Moxie said.

"Two, please," Pickle echoed.

Moxie's father scooped up the pancakes and slid them onto their plates. "Your dad just talked to a buddy from the sheriff's office, Pickle. They picked up some guys an hour ago, not far from here." He handed his daughter the syrup, and his wife joined them at the table.

"They've been watching them for a while, but couldn't ever prove anything," her father said. "These two brothers have been shipping horses out of the country for quite some time, across the border north to Canada and south to Mexico."

Moxie's father sat back and crossed his arms. "This time the sheriff and his deputies caught them red-handed, right in the middle of an illegal Mustang roundup."

"Wow!" Pickle exclaimed. "It's like in the movies!"

"Funny thing, though," Moxie's dad added. "Willie said that Sheriff Peterson and his deputies first chased the men *up* the canyon from the corral as they tried to escape. Next thing he knows, they're riding *down* the canyon to give themselves up. The guys were hollering about a grizzly bear just sitting there next to some kid on an old horse. Those tough guys were scared to death. Go figure."

Pickle gaped at Moxie's dad with a stunned look on his face. "Wow, a grizzly bear?" He turned to his best friend, who looked hard at her pancakes.

Moxie's father picked up the butter dish and offered it to his daughter, but she shook her head no. Pickle nodded yes.

"Any idea who told them about the roundup?" Moxie's mother asked as she sipped her coffee. "I heard you say the sheriff got a tip."

Moxie chewed her pancakes double-speed. Pickle's mouth hung open as he continued staring at his friend. Moxie kicked Pickle under the table, and he clamped his mouth shut.

"That's the funny thing," Moxie's father said, spreading butter on his stack. "Remember how you met Miss Laramie at the festival?" The kids nodded and looked at each other. "Well, she's training to be a sheriff's deputy in Laramie, and *she* got the tip on her cell phone."

Moxie froze. Should she just confess that she was the caller right this minute? Pickle opened his mouth to speak, but Moxie gave him another swift kick. Pickle looked at Moxie with a confused expression.

"Well, Miss Jubilee must not have known who it was," her dad said, and Moxie exhaled, relieved. "But the person called them the Jenkins gang. Nobody but the police knew that name, so she went straight to Sheriff Peterson." He reached for the maple syrup. "Peterson's office took over from there. So, we have a mysterious good citizen to thank for saving those horses."

"Do you think that person should get a reward?" Pickle's eyes narrowed as he glanced at Moxie. "If the sheriff knew who she, uh..." He hesitated and then went on. "...or he was—"

Moxie kicked him again under the table. Pickle shrugged at Moxie. "What? Why are you kicking me—"

"What was that about Officer Brown?" Moxie's mother interrupted. "I thought he was so nice."

"That's what we all thought." Her father poured syrup over the pancakes. "But get a load of this. The roadwork he told the kids about was all a lie. He wanted to keep traffic away so the trailers could pick up the horses."

"You're kidding," Moxie's mom said.

"It turns out Officer Brown was the Jenkins' lookout guy." Mr. Woodson took a sip of coffee. "Anyway, he confessed. He said he needed the money."

"Daddy, did those Jenkins guys take a lot of Mustangs?" Moxie asked.

"Seems so, kiddo. The gang had built a huge corral down the road not far from the turnoff, right in the foothills of the Snowies."

Mike Woodson dug into his pancakes, and the kids focused on theirs, too. They hoped their expressions wouldn't give away that they already knew all about the secret corral.

"That corral was filled with maybe sixty horses. They think the Mustangs are from all over this area." He paused to take another bite. "Jane, these pancakes sure hit the spot!"

"Why, thank you." Moxie's mother grinned at her daughter, and Moxie smiled back.

Her dad continued. "Remember Willie's friend, Matt Larson? He was riding through there some weeks back. He saw a Mustang herd, fifteen or twenty of them, led by a pale yellow stallion. I wonder if those horses were part of the roundup..."

Moxie was too busy eating her pancakes to talk anymore, knowing full well that those twenty Mustangs, *her* Mustangs, were safe and sound.

But what could she do to help the sixty horses that had been trapped in the Jenkins' corral? What would happen to them?

Chapter Twenty-Two

It was Monday morning, and Moxie had already fed and brushed Misty, gathered eggs, and finished her other chores when a heavy rain began to pour. She quickly discovered that the roof over her hangout in the barn had three leaks. After placing kitchen pots around the stall to catch the drips, she left Misty to her morning nap and went inside the house.

Now was the perfect time to make a cup of hot chocolate, kick off her boots, and curl up on the sofa with Bunker and a good book. She happily reread one of her favorite novels, *Black Beauty*. Every few pages, she slipped the dog a treat.

Her mother had driven into Laramie to run some errands. Her father had taken his truck to a garage in Centennial for repairs. So right now, Moxie Wyoming was in charge of Moose Creek Ranch, and she felt very grown up.

Moxie marked her page with a scrap of paper and took a sip of cocoa. She thought back to her adventure the day before and imagined Rocky and his herd of Mustangs hanging out at Dizzy Humphrey's Animal Shelter. She wondered if it was it raining there, too.

She also liked picturing the Jenkins gang galloping up to Misty with huge Grizz sitting on the rock behind them. She really loved the part where, scared to death, they turned right around to ride back to the sheriff and his deputies to surrender.

She also liked imagining Miss Jubilee Days giving the sheriff the all-important tip from the secret caller so they could catch the Jenkins Gang. Since Pickle had figured out that she was the secret caller, Moxie had made her best friend swear that he would never ever tell anyone.

She took another sip of cocoa and pulled the rodeo queen's card out of her jeans pocket. She went over to the phone and dialed.

It only took two rings. "Hello?" a friendly voice answered.

"Hi. It's Moxie Wyoming Woodson."

"Oh, I'm so happy to hear from you." Mary Lou's voice sounded like music to the young girl's ears. "You did an important thing, Moxie, leaving me that message about the Jenkins brothers. Your tip solved the case."

A smile beamed across the girl's face. "Wow, thank you, Miss Jubilee Days—"

"Moxie, call me Mary Lou."

"Uh, okay. Thank you, uh, Mary Lou, for not telling anybody my name."

"No problem. Your secret's safe with me."

"Uh, I've been thinking a lot about those Mustangs that were rounded up." Moxie took another sip of cocoa, her mind racing to figure out how she and Misty could get those sixty horses up to Dizzy's shelter.

She looked down at her magic pink cowgirl boots on the floor and flashed back to Mary Lou's shiny ruby-red boots. Were hers magic, too, and could she fly on her horse and maybe help Moxie get the sixty Mustangs to Dizzy's? Was it possible that Mary Lou was also in Dizzy's club?

But Moxie didn't know the secret password yet and didn't want to break any rules since she was a new member of Dizzy's club. She quickly decided she'd better wait before asking Mary Lou about her ruby-red boots. "Um, Mary Lou?"

"Yes?"

"What will happen to all those Mustangs?" Moxie asked.

"The government will try to find people who will adopt them. Often, families will adopt one or two horses."

"Okay..." The girl's voice drifted off.

"Hold on, I know what you're thinking, Moxie. First, keep in mind that it's a big responsibility, but if you still want to adopt a wild horse, you should talk with your parents. They can call the sheriff's office for more information."

"Thanks," Moxie said. "I'll talk to my mom and dad."

"And you call me whenever you like about anything, okay?"

"It's a deal!" And they signed off.

~~~~~

By late morning, the rain had stopped, and Moxie's parents had returned from their errands.

"Moxie Wyoming!" her mother called from outside. "Throw on your boots, and let's go for a ride with your dad."

"Great!" She pulled on her pink cowboy boots.

While her parents saddled up Captain and Skipper, Moxie leaned against her horse, struggling with the saddle's girth strap around Misty's belly. She wanted to make sure the saddle wouldn't slip to one side while she was riding. Her father stepped over to help her get the strap nice and tight.

"Ready to go, squirt?" her father asked.

"All set, Daddy," Moxie answered. "Just need to put on the bridle." She took it off a hook.

"Hold it there, young lady." Moxie's mother walked over with one arm behind her back. "I think I'll trade you that old one for this one." She brought out her hand, holding a beautiful silver bridle that she always put on Skipper.

"But, Mom!" Moxie's eyes were huge. "You won that silver bridle for your riding. I can't take that!"

"Moxie, it was always going to be yours one day." Her mother smiled. "I've decided you should have it sooner rather than later, and that Misty should wear it since she's your very own horse."

"Oh, Mom! Thank you!" Mother and daughter put the silver bridle on the little mare, who fluttered her eyelashes, feeling quite gorgeous in her shiny new jewelry.

The family rode side by side across the back pasture. The sun peeked out from behind some clouds, and the Snowies looked crystal clear in the distance.

Finally, Moxie's mother broke the silence. "I can't help but think about those Mustangs when I look up at the Snowies. I'm so glad the sheriff caught that gang."

"Yeah, sixty wild Mustangs. Beautiful horses, from what I've heard," Moxie's father said. "You know, that gang was getting ready to stuff them into trailers just as Sheriff Peterson got there."

"Well," her mom said, "it sounds like the sheriff arrived just in time to stop the whole nasty business. What a relief!"

"And I heard," Moxie added, "that the people in charge want to find good homes for those Mustangs, you know, nice people who can adopt them." She casually twirled the end of her reins. "Aaaand, Mom, Dad, we *are* nice people. Right?"

"What are you trying to say, Moxie?" Her father looked over at Moxie's mother with a smile.

Moxie sat up straight on Misty. "Dad, we're just the right kind of family to adopt a Mustang." Misty's ears perked up.

"We have enough horses, dear." Her mom adjusted the reins as Skipper threw her head around. "Besides, you already have your sweet Misty to tend to. You won't have time to take care of a new Mustang."

"I could take care of both Misty and a new Mustang friend for her," Moxie said, as Misty's ears twitched, changing direction each time another voice spoke up. "And Willie could help me train the new Mustang."

"Now, Moxie Wyoming," her dad said. "Taking on a wild horse is a big responsibility—"

"That's right, Daddy, and we should help out. The government needs lots of nice people like us to sign up and help, don'tcha think?" Moxie asked.

"Squirt, let's continue this conversation later." Her father smiled. "We're out here to ride." And with a slight kick of his boots, Mr. Woodson's mount, Captain, moved into an easy lope.

Moxie's mother was the next to take off. Skipper pranced and then launched into such a fast gallop, that Moxie's mom turned the horse in circles to slow her down. Skipper finally shifted into a smooth, comfortable trot.

Moxie watched her parents move ahead. She gave Misty a little kick with her pink boots and then, without thinking, said in a quiet voice, "Let's go."

Misty perked up and got frisky. Her gray began to fade, and she pushed off her back legs.

In the nick of time, when they were only five feet above the ground, Moxie caught herself, terrified her parents would look back and see them flying. She said with urgency, "Yikes, Misty! Not this time!"

Misty sailed down to a soft landing and the gray in her coat returned. Moxie leaned over and whispered, "We don't want them to find out our secret."

"Come on, Moxie," her dad called from ahead. "What's holding you up?"

"Be right there," Moxie shouted to him as she and Misty trotted to catch up.

~~~~~

Back from the ride, Moxie made herself a peanut butter and banana sandwich in the kitchen and found some carrots for Misty. When she left, she noticed a letter addressed to her on the front hall table. She grabbed it on her way out, stuffing it in her jeans pocket, and headed for the barn.

Dragging the desk chair from her hangout, she placed it in Misty's stall and put her sandwich on the seat. "Got something for you, girl!"

Moxie gave her mare a big kiss on the nose, scratched her fuzzy ears, and pulled the carrots from one of her pockets. "Here!"

The little horse grabbed the carrots in one swoop.

"Hey! Don't take my hand off. Easy, girl."

Misty crunched away noisily.

Moxie pulled the letter out of the other pocket, picked up her sandwich and plunked down on the chair. She took a bite of the sandwich and tore open the envelope.

"Who do you think wrote me this time?" she asked Misty.

Moxie unfolded the page, and her eyes lit up. "It's from Dizzy!" Misty stared at her, ready to listen, and Moxie read the letter out loud.

Dear Moxie Wyoming,

Good news travels fast! I heard about the capture of the Jenkins Gang. Just think, it was your phone call that led to their arrest. Don't ask me how I know all of this, but I do.

Anyway, you did a fantastic thing saving some grand Mustangs. The Pink Rose of Texas would be proud of her great-granddaughter! That's right, I knew her, too. She and Misty used to bring animals in danger to our shelter all the time.

So you see, Moxie, you're extra special, just like your Granny Rose, even if you're not a rodeo champion...yet!

I know you understand the magic of the pink boots, the power they give you when you ride Misty, and that it's important to use this power to help others. And you have! First, you and Misty rescued Rocky and his herd, who are very happy at the shelter, by the way. And then you helped save those other Mustangs from a terrible fate.

You've more than proven yourself, Moxie, and you took the oath, so you're officially on the team. I have more cases for you and Misty. You're a can-do duo!

I may even team you up with a few of our other club members—Mona Arizona, Lily Illinois, Noelia New Mexico, Diamond Duke Dakota, and Smoky Carolina are all working with us right now. When the time is right, I'll send you a secret password. You'll need it to meet up with them.

Your friend always,

Dizzy

P.S. Do you remember Pumpkin, the little beagle from North Carolina? Well, she loves Rocky and likes to sit on his back and howl "yippee-ki-yay" like a real cow dog! LOL

Chapter Twenty-Three

It was nap time at Moose Creek Ranch, and all was quiet except for two sets of gentle snores coming from inside the barn. Misty snoozed in her stall, while Moxie Wyoming did the same in hers. Still wearing the pink boots and pink riding tights, Moxie Wyoming had propped up her feet on one end of the old cot. Her hat covered her face to keep out the light.

Suddenly, Misty neighed loudly, and two sets of eyes popped open, Misty's and Moxie's. They both shook their heads to wake up.

"What's going on, Misty? Were you dreaming?" Moxie asked, still sleepy.

Then she noticed a padded brown envelope propped on the chair by her desk. "What's that?"

Moxie brought it back to her cot and examined the outside of the envelope, handling it as if it might break at any moment. It was stamped *Special Delivery* and *Confidential* several times on both sides. She glanced at the upper left corner on the front. There was no street, town, or state. She noted the letters *D.H.A.S.* written carefully. That had to be from Dizzy Humphrey's Animal Shelter.

"Misty, Dizzy sent this!" Her face lit up as she tore open the envelope. The little mare watched. "Do you think it's a present?"

Misty snorted as a small, dark-green walkie-talkie fell out of the envelope. Stuck to it was a yellow Post-it with the words *Password: Howling Red Wolf.*

"What's this?" Moxie picked it up. "This is like the big black walkie-talkie that Daddy and Willie use around the ranch when Willie's in the field and Daddy's in the barn and needs to talk to him."

The girl and the horse stared at the device.

"Except this one's smaller. And it's cuter."

She rotated one dial. It clicked, and the gadget turned on. It made a low crackling noise, startling both Moxie and Misty. "Wonder why Dizzy is sending me a walkie-talkie?"

She turned the other dial and the crackling got louder.

Moxie stared at the button on the side of the green, plastic case. "Should I press it, Misty?"

Misty pounded twice with her right hoof.

Moxie clicked the walkie-talkie and spoke into it, reading the password from the Post-it. "*Howling Red Wolf.*"

She and Misty listened as it clicked back. A girl's voice came through the hissing static.

"Moxie Wyoming, we have an emergency. Can you help?"

The Real-Life Misty & Moxie Wyoming

Nobody ever quite knew how old the real-life Misty was, but for about ten years, it was thought this small, homely, swaybacked horse was pretty close to thirty. And until she retired, the adorable Misty ruled as queen of the herd at the Darwin Guest Ranch in the Gros Ventre Mountains of western Wyoming.

Watching Misty lead the herd as it thundered into the ranch at full gallop each morning was a great way to start the day for anyone at the Darwin. After breakfast, the wrangler would saddle the horses and prep the guests for the day's activities. The little mare would do her best to push up front to lead the trail rides as queen of the Darwin visitors, too.

You always knew which horse was in and which was out by how close they stood to Misty in the corral. Over the years, the most prominent was Hector the Ejector, a huge draught-horse-mix who was Misty's protector until the end of his life—and he always stood glued to her.

One summer, Misty really did return to the Darwin Ranch from winter pasture with her son, Bandit, who became another favorite among the Darwin guests.

In 2007, it was time for Misty to retire, and she moved to a family ranch in southeastern Wyoming. When she got there, it took all of five minutes for her to bond with her new mistress, the delightful, spunky real-life, Moxie Wyoming!

So, Misty happily spent the next three years with Moxie Wyoming, riding all around her family's ranch, which at times included rounding up cows.

When they weren't out on the range, Misty hung out close to Moxie's house, munching grass and peeking in the windows for a glimpse of her beloved mistress. This was Misty's routine for the rest of her life.

When I first received the photographs of the pink-clad Moxie sitting on Misty, it planted the seed for this book. The pictures portrayed the friendship between a little girl and an ancient horse and made me ponder the make-believe possibilities of their partnership.

What would happen if those pink cowgirl boots that Moxie wore in the photograph were magical? Couldn't a slight kick transform Misty into her younger self, now able to fly the two of them to all sorts of adventures? I imagined them, the way Dizzy Humphrey does in the story, as the ultimate can-do duo!

The real Misty gave the real Moxie Wyoming and everyone who met her many years of happiness. Now she will give readers the same joy through her enchanted story.

Niki Danforth, January 2015

Moxie Wyoming Sigel and Misty, November, 2007 shortly after Misty's arrival at the Hecht Creek Ranch.

Mustangs

People all across America regard Mustangs as a symbol of freedom and beauty.

Mustangs come from Spanish stock brought to the Americas by the Conquistadors starting in the sixteenth century. Some of these sturdy little horses escaped into the wild, where they came to be called Mustangs, originating from the Spanish word *mesteño*, meaning horse without an owner. Mustangs found a great environment in the American West, and eventually there were more than two million wild horses roaming the plains.

Then ranchers settled these same areas and considered the Mustangs a nuisance. They believed the horses competed with their cattle for the grasses, and so the numbers of horses rapidly declined. A very well-known lady named Velma Johnston, better known as *Wild Horse Annie*, fought to save the Mustangs with the help of thousands of children writing to Congress. Finally, in 1971 she got Congress to pass *The Free Roaming Wild Horse and Burro Act*, giving protection to these tough horses. The management for the horses was given to the Bureau of Land Management, a federal government agency.

These mostly small, rugged creatures run in what is called family bands and have a very strict and loving social structure. The stallion is the protector of the band, and always takes the position in the herd between the family and any potential danger. The family also has a lead mare who is trusted to guide the family away from danger and to a safe place. All the members of the family band watch over and love their offspring, or the babies.

Young males are kicked out of the family at around age two, and usually join a few other young males. This group is referred to as a bachelor band. They will roam together, acting like a bunch of teenage boys, until they become strong enough to steal a female mare or two and start their own band. The young females will usually leave the family when they are between two and three years old, and either join a different band or go with a young bachelor.

Mustangs are considered a flight or fight animal. This means they will always try to run away from danger, and will only fight if they are cornered. Mustangs are wild, but when not threatened, they can become very curious about people. They share many traits with human beings, such as creating a family structure that includes a love of family. And like people, they also have the ability to socialize and establish friendships with other horses.

Today in the United States, there are less than fifty-thousand Mustangs still running wild in the entire country. Because of the years I have spent helping them and witnessing what is happening as their numbers dwindle, I find the biggest problem is mismanagement of these horses that are, by law, supposed to be protected.

I worry that the time will come when the only place that you might get to see wild mustangs will be at a sanctuary or refuge. Still, there is something magical about the experience of watching them, even at a refuge. There are fine sanctuaries, such as Return To Freedom in California, Black Hills Wild Horse Sanctuary in South Dakota, and Pryor Mountain Wild Mustang Center in Wyoming, and their links are listed below.

Most of all, people really love seeing these horses free and happy with their bands. These animals have been our important partners as we've settled this country. We are losing a priceless heritage.

This article was written by Sandi Claypool, founder of Monero Mustangs.

Here are some Mustang websites to visit.
Return To Freedom:
http://www.returntofreedom.org/

Black Hills Wild Horse Sanctuary:
http://www.wildmustangs.com/

Pryor Mountain Wild Mustang Center:
www.pryormustangs.org

The Grizzly Bear

To many, the grizzly bear is the true symbol of the wilderness. A top predator that generally avoids people and requires vast expanses of the wildest country in the world, a grizzly is an impressive and awesome creature by anyone's standards. This is a mammal that commands true respect, since an adult male bear may weigh as much as 800 pounds and females much less.

Most of what a grizzly bear does is driven by its constant search for food. He or she will cover considerable distances for a favorite food, as much as twenty to thirty miles at times. The bear is omnivorous, meaning it will eat both plants and animals. Although a notorious predator, a grizzly is primarily a vegetarian, with as much as ninety percent of its diet based on plants.

In early springtime, after emerging from their dens, grizzlies will follow their excellent sense of smell to locate the carcasses of big game animals such as moose, elk, and deer that have died during the winter. As plants begin to green up, they will graze on grasses and other plants at lower elevations in valleys. As spring turns to summer, these bears will generally follow the rising snow line and the greening vegetation to the higher elevations.

During the summer, grizzly bears forage, or feed, on grasses and roots in high alpine meadows and catch small mammals occasionally, such as ground squirrels. As summer turns to fall, a number of bears can be found rolling over rocks on high-elevation slopes of rock debris to feed on army cutworm moths. The nuts found in whitebark pine cones are another important fall food. Squirrels hide the cones on the forest floor, and grizzly bears raid these stored foods when they find them. Also, many bears will take advantage of a variety of berries, such as chokecherry, serviceberry, currant and hawthorn, as they ripen at the lower elevations in late summer and fall.

Although grizzly bears are not true hibernators (like amphibians that do not wake up for months), they do spend most of the winter sleeping in a den. Bears typically dig their own dens and head in for the winter in early November. During denning, their heart rate drops, breathing slows, and body temperature goes down. All of their bodily functions slow to reduce demands on the stored food supply in their bodies. Over winter, they may lose twenty to thirty percent of their body weight. After sleeping for several months, their muscles are still nearly as strong as when they went into their dens. Humans would lose nearly all their muscle strength in that period of inactivity.

A female grizzly bear, called a sow, will usually have between one and three cubs while in the den in late January or early February. When born, cubs are roughly a foot long and weigh about one pound. They are born helpless, nearly hairless, and with closed eyes. The cubs will nurse on their mother's milk while in the den and well after they emerge from the den, typically in April.

Most young grizzlies will spend another two full years with their mother, learning how to forage and avoid hazards (usually associated with people or adult male grizzlies), before heading out on their own. Grizzlies are known to live a long time, and some survive as long as thirty years.

While grizzly bears generally choose to avoid people, they are powerful—even dangerous—animals, especially when surprised or when they feel they must protect something, such as their cubs or a food source. Therefore, if we encounter a bear while out hiking, it is always important to give the animal a lot of space so it does not feel threatened.

It is also important that we always take good care of our food and garbage, or anything else a bear may want to eat. For those living in bear country, garbage should always be stored in a bear resistant garbage can in a secure building before pick-up. While camping, food should be made unavailable by storing it in a vehicle while away or hanging it in a tree at least ten feet above the ground and four feet away from the tree trunk. A bear that begins to associate food with people soon becomes very dangerous.

Fortunately, most encounters with bears work out just fine. The bear simply goes about its business and we get a nice wildlife viewing experience. Peaceful coexistence between humans and bears depends on our respect and responsibility.

No other wild animal in North America captures our imagination the way the grizzly bear does. Some people see bears as cute and cuddly. Others see them as fierce and terrifying. The truth is they are simply wild animals doing their best to survive just like all creatures in nature.

They need vast areas of undisturbed wilderness, which means there will likely never be a large number of grizzly bears on the landscape. With an ever-increasing number of humans in our world, providing the space grizzlies need will continue to be a challenge. The future of the grizzly bear is squarely in our hands.

This article was written by Mark Gocke, who is a Public Information Specialist with the Wyoming Game and Fish Department. He has lived in the heart of grizzly country for nearly twenty years, in Jackson Hole, Wyoming.

Acknowledgements

A Wild Ride: The Adventures of Misty & Moxie Wyoming would still be just an idea without the kindness and support of numerous people. My gratitude to the following for their help:

the extraordinary Sigel family—Harmony, Ed, Moxie and Gus—without them, there would be no novel;

G. Miki Hayden, a most thorough and patient editor, and Mercy Pilkington, who critiqued and edited the novel and goes the distance for her writers;

wonderful friends who served as an informal focus group along the way, including Loring Woodman, who owned the Darwin Ranch for forty years where Misty spent most of her life; water colorist Karen Bruett, who served as a visual sounding board for the novel; horse expert Annah Otis; and Jane Ely, Cindy Grogan, and Helen Zax, the best brainstorming partners a writer could hope for;

a very special book club of young readers in Bernardsville, New Jersey, who provided valuable input early on: Catie Sharp, Charlotte Depew, Cassidy Meeks, and Natalie Fischer, and their moms, who not only coordinated their daughters' book club, but gave story input, too: Lynn Sharp, Georgiana Depew, Maureen Meeks, Denise Fischer;

and finally, Dan, who encourages my writing and storytelling and believes in me.

Niki Danforth, January 2015

Author

Niki Danforth rode the real-life Misty for many years at the Darwin Ranch in Wyoming. When it was time for this marvelous mare to retire, Danforth moved her to another ranch where Misty met Moxie Wyoming. The friendship between the girl and the little horse inspired the author to write this story.

A Note from the Author

Thank you very much for taking the time to read *A Wild Ride: The Adventures of Misty & Moxie Wyoming*. As a writer, I love receiving feedback on my characters and stories. Also, I've lost track of the number of times that my novel has been reread to catch any mistakes. Should you spot a typo or wish to share other thoughts about Moxie Wyoming and her world, please email me at nikidanforth5@gmail.com. I'd love to hear from you.

Reviews are important to Indie Authors, so please consider writing one about *A Wild Ride* on your favorite eBook retailer or review site.

To hear all the latest news about Moxie Wyoming and other future Niki Danforth books, please sign up at http://nikidanforth.com/ for a newsletter.

All my best,
Niki

Made in the USA
Middletown, DE
22 May 2019